P. Croft is a celebrated author of young adult and children's fiction, best known for her captivating stories that combine action, suspense, and relatable characters. In the first book of *The Teenage Spy* collection, she introduces readers to Emily Carter, a bold and brilliant teenage spy navigating the thrills and challenges of espionage and young love.

When she's not writing, she enjoys exploring new destinations, indulging in mystery novels, and creating stories that inspire and entertain readers of all ages. She resides in Canada with her husband.

The Weekend Spy

By: P. Croft

Chapter 1

"Tell me you're joking, Benson. I just sat down in algebra." Emily whispered into her phone, the fluorescent lights of the school bathroom flickering overhead. Her voice was low, urgent, blending with the buzz of voices just beyond the stall door.

"Wish I could, Carter," came the dry reply. "This mission can't wait. Intel confirms a handoff happening in Paris tonight. You need to intercept."

Emily squeezed her eyes shut, pressing her back against the cold tiled wall. The faint smell of lavender soap did little to soothe her pounding heart. "Tonight? Are you serious? I have a history test tomorrow and Mrs. Klein already hates me."

A pause crackled through the line, and then Benson's voice softened, a rare moment of levity. "I'm sure Mrs. Klein will survive. But the world won't if that microchip slips through our fingers. You're the best we've got."

Before Emily could respond, the bathroom door swung open, and a chorus of laughter burst in. Emily stiffened, forcing herself to sound casual as she muttered, "Fine. Send me the details."

She hung up, tucking her phone into her backpack as she adjusted her reflection in the cracked mirror. Her heart still raced, the anticipation and fear blending into the same familiar rush. The reflection staring back at her was that of a 14-year-old girl with messy auburn hair and a twinge of nervous energy—but beneath that, she was a spy, ready to slip into her second life.

"Paris," she whispered to herself, a smile tugging at her lips. "Here we go again."

Emily tapped her pencil against her open history textbook, eyes darting back and forth as she tried to absorb information on ancient civilizations. The classroom was filled with the soft murmurs of students, the occasional cough, and the rhythmic clicking of a pencil from somewhere behind her.

The harsh fluorescent lights hummed overhead, casting a sterile glow on the room's scuffed linoleum floors and graffiti-scarred desks.

On the wall, a faded poster of famous explorers seemed to watch her with bemused expressions.

"Emily! Did you hear a word I just said?" Sophie's voice snapped her out of her thoughts. Her best friend sat next to her, eyebrow raised and lips twisted in a mixture of amusement and exasperation.

Emily blinked, quickly turning her attention back to Sophie. "Uh, yeah! Totally," she said, nodding a bit too enthusiastically. She felt the heat rise in her cheeks as Sophie narrowed her eyes.

"Right," Sophie drawled, leaning back in her chair and crossing her arms. She was wearing her favorite oversized hoodie, the one with the "Save the Bees" slogan printed across the front. Sophie had a way of making even the most casual attire look chic, her dark curls pulled back into a high ponytail that bounced with every skeptical tilt of her head.

Emily sighed, glancing down at the textbook. "Sorry, Soph. Just distracted," she admitted. That much was true, although not for the reasons Sophie might think. The blue folder tucked into her backpack weighed heavily on her mind.

Inside, encrypted mission details waited for her—the real kind of history that would never make it into Mr. Blanchard's syllabus.

"You've been 'distracted' all week," Sophie said, mock-quoting the air with her fingers. "Seriously, what gives? Is it Alex? I swear if he's being a jerk again, I'll—"

Emily couldn't help the laugh that bubbled up. "No, no, nothing like that," she said quickly, raising her hands as if to deflect Sophie's well-meaning wrath. The classroom chatter dimmed slightly as Mr. Blanchard stood at the front, adjusting his thick glasses and clearing his throat.

"Eyes up front, people," he said, his voice as dry as the chalk he wrote with. He turned to scrawl the day's topic on the board: The Great Wall of China: A Symbol of Power and Perseverance. The screech of the chalk made Emily wince, but she took the opportunity to glance at the large clock on the wall. Two more hours until school ended and she could go "home"—or rather, to the covert agency's safe house disguised as a dry cleaning business.

The ticking of the clock seemed louder now, each second stretching out painfully. Sophie leaned in, whispering conspiratorially, "Don't think I don't notice that look in your eye.

It's the same one you had before you bailed on movie night last month."

Emily's mind raced, a smile flickering across her lips despite the anxiety bubbling beneath her surface. "What look? I don't have a look."

"Emily, please. If you get any more mysterious, you're going to start wearing a trench coat and talking in code."

If only you knew, Emily thought. She stifled a laugh, pretending to scribble notes as Mr. Blanchard turned around and scanned the class. He raised an eyebrow at her, suspicious as always when she appeared too entertained. She made a show of frowning at her textbook, hoping he'd move on. He did, and she exhaled, stealing a glance at Sophie, who was still watching her like a detective piecing together a crime.

Outside the window, the late afternoon sun cast warm, dappled light over the school's courtyard, where students lounged on benches, oblivious to anything more exciting than last night's homework.

Emily's heart ached for the simplicity of their lives, where the only double life was pretending not to care about test scores.

"Soon," she whispered to herself, eyes darting back to the clock. The weekend was almost here, and while her classmates would be heading to sleepovers and soccer games, she'd be slipping into a disguise and boarding a flight to who-knows-where.

Sophie tilted her head, catching the whispered word. "Soon what?" she asked, raising an eyebrow.
"Soon… we'll get ice cream after school?" Emily offered, her smile wide and a touch too bright. Sophie laughed, shaking her head as the bell rang, and Emily's heart raced —not just from relief, but from the thrill of knowing that, in a few hours, her real life would begin again.

Chapter 2

Emily Carter's heart thudded in her chest as she sat on her bed, carefully arranging her backpack so that her parents wouldn't see the agency-issued gadgets hidden beneath layers of clothes and books. The soft glow of her desk lamp cast shadows across the room, highlighting the framed photos of her family vacations and school friends. Her parents knocked gently before opening the door, their faces etched with the usual concern.

"You all set for your academic retreat?" her mom asked, a warm smile crinkling the corners of her eyes. Emily's dad stood just behind, arms crossed but eyes soft.

"Yep! I'll be back Sunday evening," Emily said, forcing cheerfulness into her voice. "It's supposed to be all study, study, study, but at least it'll look good on college applications."

Her dad chuckled. "Our little overachiever. Just be careful, all right? Stay with the group and call us if anything happens."

"I will," Emily promised, guilt gnawing at her as she hugged them both. The truth was, they had no idea she was about to slip into a life far removed from exams and essays.

An hour later, Emily was at the airport, the low hum of voices and the beeping of boarding calls filling the air. Her agency contact, Benson, had sent her the flight details just after she'd left the house. Disguised as a typical student on a weekend trip, Emily breezed through check-in and security, her heart pounding when the agent glanced at her passport a moment too long. But then came the metallic click of the stamp, and she was through.

Just another part of the plan, she reminded herself as she boarded the plane. The briefing Benson had sent burned in her mind: High-profile gala at the Palais des Lumières. Retrieve microchip from statue. Rival agents expected. Use extreme caution.

Emily settled into her seat by the window, the Paris-bound jet thrumming beneath her. The city's night lights awaited her, but her thoughts momentarily drifted to Sophie's last text.

Sophie: Sooo sad you're missing the sleepover! Zoe's bringing the weird face masks again. You better tell me everything about your weekend "retreat" when you're back!

Emily bit her lip and typed back quickly.

Emily: Trust me, nothing exciting. Just boring lectures and too much homework. Save a face mask for me!

The guilt was there, a constant companion. Sophie had no idea that Emily's "boring" weekend was anything but.

The jet's engines roared to life, and Emily leaned back, gazing out the window as the plane lifted into the sky. Her reflection stared back at her, eyes wide with a mixture of anticipation and nerves.

Paris welcomed her with a crisp breeze and the smell of rain-soaked cobblestones. A sleek black car waited at the curb, its driver—a tall man in a crisp suit—gave her a nod as she approached.

"Mademoiselle Carter," he said, opening the door.

"Merci," she replied, slipping in. The interior smelled faintly of leather and pine, and as they wove through the narrow, lamp-lit streets of Paris, Emily's mind replayed the briefing.

The statue holds the microchip. Rival agents will be watching. Stay sharp.

The car pulled up to the Palais des Lumières, its grand façade illuminated by spotlights. The air buzzed with laughter, music, and the clinking of champagne glasses. Emily stepped out, smoothing the skirt of her midnight blue gown. She was not used to dresses, let alone ones that sparkled under the Parisian sky, but tonight demanded it
.

Her entrance was seamless, her eyes scanning the room beneath the pretense of admiring the ornate chandeliers and gilded walls. The statue was at the far end, surrounded by velvet ropes and watched by guards who looked more interested in their phones than their duty.

"Well, this might be easier than I thought," she whispered, a small smile playing on her lips.
"May I offer you a drink?" a voice purred behind her. She turned, her smile freezing when she saw him—Lucas Dupont.
Tall, with tousled dark hair and eyes that gleamed with a mischievous spark. He was new at the agency, assigned to missions she didn't quite trust.
"Lucas," she said, tilting her head with a smirk. "Didn't think you'd show."

"Where there's trouble, there's me," he said, his grin widening. The hint of flirtation in his voice sent a shiver down her spine, equal parts unsettling and thrilling.

"Let's hope you're not here to make it harder," she muttered, eyeing him as he slipped away into the crowd. Focus, Emily.

She reached the statue and knelt, pretending to adjust the strap of her shoe. Her fingers worked quickly, slipping the micro-laser from her clutch and slicing through the glass case. The soft hum of the device blended with the music, but her heart thumped wildly as she felt eyes on her back.

"A little far from home, aren't we?" Lucas's voice whispered, closer now. She glanced over her shoulder, catching the glint of playful challenge in his eyes.
"Don't blow this," she whispered back, the microchip slipping into her pocket. He raised an eyebrow, his smirk deepening.

"After you," he said, stepping back as she made for the exit. Shouts erupted behind them—Volkov, a rival agent, had spotted them.
Emily sprinted, heels clattering on the marble floor. Lucas was beside her, his laughter mingling with the chaos. What is wrong with him? she thought, exasperated but secretly amused.
They burst onto the rooftop, the Parisian skyline stretching before them, the Eiffel Tower's lights winking in the distance.

"Jump or be caught," Lucas said, grabbing her hand.

"Au revoir," Emily muttered, squeezing his hand as they leapt into the night, the wind roaring past them as a helicopter's rope ladder swung into view.

The rush of air stung her face, and for a split second, the world seemed suspended—all sparkling lights and dizzying heights. Her fingers caught the rope ladder, the rough material biting into her palms. Lucas landed beside her, gripping the rungs with a practiced ease, his dark hair whipped by the wind.

"Nice of you to join me," he shouted over the roar.

Emily couldn't help but laugh, adrenaline still coursing through her veins. "You better not slow me down next time."

"As if," Lucas replied, his grin widening as the helicopter surged upward, carrying them into the safety of the night sky.

"Nice timing, Benson," she gasped into her comms, a laugh bubbling up despite herself.

"Anything for you, Carter," Benson's voice crackled through the headset, tinged with a hint of relief.

As Paris shrank below them, Emily glanced sideways at Lucas, who was watching her with an expression she couldn't quite read. It was somewhere between amusement and admiration. She felt her cheeks warm, the thrill of the mission mingling with a new, unexpected excitement.

This weekend just got more complicated.

Emily's arrival back home was marked by the first rays of dawn slicing through the sky. The agency's jet landed smoothly, and before long, she was in a car headed to the debriefing. The city streets were quiet, and the soft glow of streetlights began to fade as morning took over.

The safe house, disguised as an old brick building, was nondescript from the outside. Inside, Benson sat at a polished table, fingers steepled as he watched Emily step in. "Mission report," he said, his voice even.

Emily recounted the night, omitting the details of Lucas's unexpected appearance. She detailed the gala, the microchip retrieval, and the chaotic escape. Benson nodded, his eyes narrowing at the mention of Volkov

"Good work, Carter. Go home, rest up," he said, a rare hint of approval in his tone.

By the time Emily slipped into her house, the sun was beginning to warm the horizon. She crept through the front door, wincing at the soft creak of the hinges. The familiar scent of coffee brewing drifted from the kitchen, and her mom's voice floated in from around the corner.

"Emily? Is that you?"

Emily's heart skipped. She took a breath and stepped into the kitchen. Her mom stood by the counter, a steaming mug in hand, her eyes still sleepy but alert with motherly concern.

"Hey, Mom," Emily said, forcing a casual tone. "I got back a little early. The last session ended sooner than expected."

Her mom's eyes softened with relief. "I'm glad you're home safe. Did you get any sleep?"
"A little," Emily lied, offering a smile. "I think I'm going to head up and crash for a bit."

"Of course, sweetheart. Get some rest," her mom said, stepping forward to plant a kiss on Emily's forehead. "We'll catch up later."

Emily nodded, exhaustion beginning to weigh down her limbs as she trudged up the stairs. Her room was exactly as she'd left it—warm and familiar. She dropped her bag by the bed and sank into the mattress, the events of the past night replaying in vivid detail.
Just as she closed her eyes, her phone buzzed. She groaned but reached for it, expecting another agency message.
Instead, it was Sophie.

Sophie: EMILY! Emergency! Call me when you wake up! You will NOT believe what happened at the sleepover.
A tired smile tugged at Emily's lips. Despite the secret life she led, moments like this grounded her. She typed back:
Emily: Give me an hour. Can't wait to hear all about it.

With that, she set her phone down and let the comfort of her room pull her into sleep, knowing that, for now, she was just Emily Carter—student, friend, and spy, trying to balance it all.

Chapter 3

The first bell rang out across the crowded halls of Riverton High, signaling the start of another long day. Emily Carter's exhaustion had only deepened overnight, and her body felt leaden as she moved to her first class. She pushed open the heavy door of the history classroom and was met with Mr. Blanchard's stern gaze.

"Miss Carter," he said, not bothering to mask his annoyance. His squinting eyes locked on her as he set down a stack of papers. "You missed the test on Friday."

Emily shifted uncomfortably under his scrutiny. "I know, Mr. Blanchard. I'm sorry about that—the academic retreat —"

He raised a hand, cutting her off. "Save it. You'll be taking it now. I hope you're prepared."

She nodded, a lump forming in her throat as the other students whispered behind her. Sophie, sitting a few rows away, gave her a subtle look of concern. Emily made her way to an empty desk at the front and sank into the chair. Mr. Blanchard handed her the test with a flourish, the rustle of the pages sounding louder than it should.

"You have until the end of the period," he said, his voice flat.

The classroom buzzed around her as she stared at the first question. Explain the key points of the Treaty of Versailles. The words blurred for a moment, and she forced herself to focus. She could still feel the ache in her arms from clinging to the helicopter ladder, and the bruises on her sides throbbed with every breath.

Minutes ticked by, the sound of pencils scratching against paper echoing in her ears. She pushed through the fog of fatigue, jotting down answers with practiced precision. When she glanced up, Mr. Blanchard was watching her, his gaze calculating.

The bell finally rang, signaling the end of the period. Emily stood to hand in her paper, her legs shaky but steady enough.

"We'll see how well that retreat prepared you," Mr. Blanchard muttered, taking the test from her hand.

Emily mustered a weak smile. "Thank you, Mr. Blanchard."

"We'll talk if your answers don't match your potential," he added, his voice trailing behind her as she exited the room.

———

Afternoon sunlight streamed through the tall windows of the gym as Emily stepped into the locker room. The chatter of her teammates bounced off the tile walls, and the air was thick with the familiar scent of sweat and deodorant. Emily changed into her basketball practice uniform, wincing as she pulled her shirt over her head and felt the tug on the bruises lining her ribs.

"Whoa, Emily, what happened there?" Kayla, a sharp-eyed junior with a knack for gossip, pointed to the dark purple marks peeking out from under her sports bra.

Emily's heart skipped, and she struggled to keep her face neutral. "Oh, just… slipped on some stairs at the retreat," she said, forcing a laugh.

Kayla's eyebrows shot up. "Looks pretty rough for just a slip," she said, glancing sideways at another girl who snickered.

Before Emily could respond, Sophie—who had just walked in—stepped up, her eyes darting between the girls and Emily. "Yeah, they're brutal at those academic camps," Sophie said with a smile that was just sharp enough to shut down the whispers. "I mean, did you hear about the mandatory dodgeball tournament?"

The girls laughed, some rolling their eyes before turning back to their lockers. The tension eased, and Emily shot Sophie a grateful look.

"Thanks," Emily whispered as they walked to the court together.

Sophie's smile faded as they reached the gym doors. "Em, we need to talk. Those bruises… they're not from any academic retreat, are they?"

Emily hesitated, the weight of her double life pressing down on her like never before. "Sophie, I—"

Before she could finish, Coach Parker's whistle pierced the air. "Let's go, ladies! On the court!"

"Later," Emily said, the promise hanging between them as they joined the team. Sophie's eyes were clouded with worry, and Emily knew that avoiding this conversation wouldn't be possible for much longer.

Practice was grueling, each sprint and drill sending jolts of pain through her battered body. But Emily pushed through, determined to keep up appearances. By the time the final whistle blew, she was drenched in sweat and aching all over.

As the team filed out, Emily reached for her phone in her bag. A new message lit up the screen:

Lucas: Hope school isn't too boring without a rooftop escape. Take care of those bruises.

A smile flickered across her lips, a mix of frustration and warmth filling her chest. Sophie caught the look and frowned.

"Em, who is that?"
Emily locked her phone and met her best friend's gaze. "It's complicated," she said softly.

Sophie's expression shifted from suspicion to concern. "Well, I'm here when you're ready to explain."
Emily nodded, the noise of the gym fading as she let out a sigh. She was balancing on the thinnest of wires, and one misstep could send everything crashing down.

Sophie's eyes searched hers for a moment before she nodded, though the tension between them lingered like a storm cloud.
Emily walked home under the amber glow of the streetlights, the chill of autumn biting at her cheeks. She glanced at her phone one last time, Lucas's message still glowing on the screen.

This life is getting harder to balance, she thought, a mix of dread and anticipation swirling within her.
When she finally stepped through her front door, her mom called out from the living room. "Emily, is that you? How was school?"

"Yeah, it's me," Emily replied, forcing energy into her voice. "School was fine. Just tired."

"Get some rest," her mom said, eyes softening with concern. "Dinner will be in an hour."

Emily nodded and trudged up the stairs to her room. She sat on the edge of her bed, staring at the darkened screen of her phone. A text from Lucas and the subtle ache of Sophie's suspicion weighed on her. She exhaled, flopping back onto her pillows.

Before she could drift off, her phone buzzed once more. This time, it was Sophie.

Sophie: I'm here if you want to talk. Just worried about you.

Tears pricked the corners of Emily's eyes. She typed back slowly.

Emily: I know. Thanks, Soph. I'll explain soon. Promise.

She set the phone aside, the tension in her chest easing just a bit. For now, she was caught between two worlds—and she could only hope she wouldn't lose either.

The rest of the school week passed in a blur of homework, classes, and stolen moments of exhaustion. Each day felt heavier than the last, and Emily found herself nodding off in the middle of lectures. On Wednesday, she barely caught herself before slipping into a nap during a pop quiz in Math. Mr. Carson's sharp, suspicious glance was enough to keep her awake for the rest of the period.

Lunch periods became a reprieve, where the noise of the cafeteria masked the anxious thrum of thoughts in her head. Sophie was by her side, more watchful than usual. Emily noticed the way Sophie's eyes lingered on her when she thought Emily wasn't looking. The tension of unspoken questions hung between them like a thick fog.

By Thursday, the school buzzed with excitement. The upcoming dance had everyone talking, and the hallways were filled with bursts of laughter and whispered plans. Posters with glittering letters that read "Spring Fling" were plastered on every bulletin board.

"So, are you going?" Sophie asked as they sat at their usual lunch table. She poked at her salad with a plastic fork, her eyes darting to Emily's for a response.

Emily forced a smile. "I don't know. I'm probably going to be busy that weekend." The truth was, she had no idea if another mission would pull her away.

Sophie rolled her eyes dramatically. "You're always busy. Come on, Em, it's just one night. You deserve some fun." Before Emily could reply, a loud cheer erupted from the other side of the cafeteria.

"No way," Sophie whispered, her eyes widening as she watched Matt Turner—tall, athletic, and the captain of the basketball team—approach their table. Emily's pulse quickened, sensing the drama about to unfold.

"Hey, Sophie," Matt said, a confident grin lighting up his face.

 The cafeteria seemed to quiet, heads turning as whispers rippled through the room. "I was wondering if you'd like to go to the Spring Fling with me?"

Sophie's eyes went wide, and a blush crept up her cheeks. Emily watched her friend's shock shift into a broad, disbelieving smile.

"I'd—I'd love to," Sophie stammered, her voice barely above a whisper.

The cafeteria erupted with excited chatter, and Emily felt a rush of warmth for her friend. Sophie's joy was infectious, and for a moment, the weight on Emily's shoulders lifted.

"Looks like you're going to that dance after all," Emily teased, nudging Sophie as Matt walked away with a triumphant wave.

Sophie turned to Emily, eyes sparkling. "I can't believe this. You have to come with me, Em. We'll find you a dress, and we'll make it a night to remember."

Emily's smile faltered for a split second, but she nodded. "We'll see," she said, hoping it would be enough to appease Sophie.

Throughout the week, Lucas's texts appeared at unexpected moments, each one making Emily's heart flutter in ways she hadn't anticipated.

Lucas: How's life as a high school hero? Save any history tests lately?

Emily: Only narrowly. High school might be tougher than missions.

Lucas: Let me know if you need a rooftop escape plan.

Emily chuckled to herself, the exchange bringing a welcome burst of light to her day. But with each message, the lines between her two lives blurred, and she felt the pull of both worlds more strongly.

On Friday, just before the last bell, Emily stood by her locker, organizing her books for the weekend. The hallways buzzed with students making plans for the dance, laughter and shouts echoing down the corridor.

Her phone vibrated in her pocket, and she pulled it out, expecting another playful message from Lucas. Instead, the text was different.

Lucas: Be careful, Emily. There's talk of Volkov sniffing around again. Watch your back.

A shiver ran down her spine. The carefree noise of the school hall seemed to fade into the background as the weight of Lucas's warning settled over her.

"Hey, Em, you okay?" Sophie's voice broke through her thoughts. She stood there, her brows knit with concern.

Emily forced a smile, shoving the phone back into her pocket. "Yeah, just tired."

Sophie's eyes softened, but there was a flicker of doubt. "Well, don't forget, we're picking out your dress tomorrow. You promised."

Emily nodded, the sense of normalcy Sophie offered a lifeline she couldn't refuse. "I won't forget," she said, her voice steady, even as her mind raced with questions she couldn't voice.

Chapter 4

Emily Carter awoke to the faint hum of her phone vibrating under her pillow. Bleary-eyed, she fumbled for it, squinting at the screen as the agency's logo glowed in the pre-dawn darkness. Her heart kicked into overdrive. A new mission.

Subject: Shanghai - High Priority Mission Objective: Infiltrate the offices of tech magnate Wei Ling. Extract data on AI project codenamed "Sentinel," potentially dangerous capabilities. Operative Lucas Dupont assigned as backup. Be cautious: Ling's security is tight.

Emily sat up, adrenaline washing away the remnants of sleep. The sound of rain tapping against her window filled the silence of her room. The faint glow of the streetlights cast long shadows across her desk, where textbooks and unfinished assignments lay waiting. Another weekend of pretending.

She took a deep breath before heading downstairs, rehearsing her story in her mind. In the kitchen, her mom was already sipping her morning coffee, eyes flitting over the newspaper.

"Morning, Mom," Emily said, slipping into her practiced nonchalance.
"Morning, sweetheart. You're up early," her mom said, raising an eyebrow.

"Yeah," Emily feigned a sheepish grin. "I forgot to tell you, the academic program is hosting a last-minute workshop in tech and innovation. It's... out of town," she added, hoping the vague detail would slide by unnoticed.
Her mom's eyes narrowed slightly. "Out of town? Where?"
"San Francisco," Emily said, choosing a location far enough to justify her absence but not so exotic as to arouse suspicion. "It's a great opportunity. Lots of hands-on experience."

There was a pause before her mom's shoulders relaxed. "Well, just be careful. I trust you, Em, but you've been traveling so much. Don't burn yourself out."
Emily's heart squeezed. "I won't, I promise."

Upstairs, she sent a quick text to Sophie before heading to pack.

Emily: Last-minute academic trip. Back late Sunday. Let's hang Monday?

Almost immediately, Sophie's reply came through.

Sophie: Ugh, AGAIN? You owe me big time! Be safe.

Emily smiled at her best friend's dramatic response. The guilt gnawed at her, but she pushed it aside. There was no room for it now.

———

The briefing room at the agency safe house was dimly lit, and the air buzzed with a quiet tension. Benson stood at the front, his eyes sharp behind wire-rimmed glasses.

"Wei Ling's Sentinel project has the potential to upend global security. Its AI capabilities could destabilize entire networks. Emily, you'll go in as a delivery worker," Benson said, clicking through surveillance photos of Ling's towering office building in Shanghai.

"And me?" Lucas's familiar voice came from behind Emily. She didn't turn, but her pulse quickened. He moved to stand beside her, the warmth of his presence unsettling her composure.

"You'll be inside as an IT consultant," Benson continued. "Ensure Emily's extraction goes smoothly. Your cover will be thin, so timing is everything."

"Wei Ling's Sentinel project has the potential to upend global security. Its AI capabilities could destabilize entire networks. Emily, you'll go in as a delivery worker," Benson said, clicking through surveillance photos of Ling's towering office building in Shanghai.

"And me?" Lucas's familiar voice came from behind Emily. She didn't turn, but her pulse quickened. He moved to stand beside her, the warmth of his presence unsettling her composure.

"You'll be inside as an IT consultant," Benson continued. "Ensure Emily's extraction goes smoothly. Your cover will be thin, so timing is everything."

Lucas shot her a sideways glance, his lips quirking up in a grin. "Looks like we're partners again."
Emily's heartbeat stuttered. She focused on Benson's voice, trying to ignore the way Lucas's voice resonated in her chest.
"Remember," Benson said, his tone dropping, "Ling's guards aren't just muscle. They're trained to spot inconsistencies. One slip, and you're compromised."

Emily swallowed hard. The stakes were higher than ever, and the added layer of Lucas's presence complicated everything.

The memory of his hand gripping hers on the rooftop in Paris sent an involuntary shiver down her spine.

——

The bustling streets of Shanghai were a world apart from Riverton High. Neon lights and the chatter of passersby blurred into a symphony of urban life. Dressed in the plain uniform of a delivery worker, Emily pushed a cart loaded with boxes marked with fake tech company logos. Her heart thumped as she approached the side entrance of Ling's building.

Lucas's voice came through the earpiece. "Looking good, Carter."

"Focus," she whispered, though a smile played at her lips.

"I am," he replied, his voice lower. The unspoken words lingered, sparking warmth beneath her practiced calm.

Inside, the polished marble floors and glass walls reflected Emily's tense expression. She wheeled the cart past reception, nodding at a disinterested guard. Every step took her deeper into the labyrinthine office.

In the elevator, she caught her breath, eyes flicking to the small security camera in the corner. Lucas's voice hummed in her ear. "You're clear for now. The server room is on the 18th floor."

The doors opened with a soft ding, and Emily stepped out, heart hammering. She navigated the sterile hallway, the hum of servers growing louder. Just as she found the mainframe, footsteps echoed behind her.

"Hey! What are you doing here?" a guard barked.
Emily spun around, her mind racing. "Oh! Delivery for IT," she said, lifting a box with an awkward smile. "They said they needed these right away."
The guard's eyes narrowed. "I didn't hear about any delivery."
Lucas's voice buzzed urgently. "Stay calm."

Emily's eyes darted to the guard's badge. "Maybe you could check with Mr. Liu?" she said, dropping the name Benson had given her. She forced a laugh. "They'd throw me under the bus if I delay this."

The guard's suspicion wavered, and he lifted his radio. Before he could speak, another voice cut in from the shadows.

"I'll take it from here," said a girl Emily's age, her dark eyes sharp and confident.
Emily's brows shot up as the girl stepped forward. "Name's Mei," she said under her breath. "You're going to need help getting out."

Surprise flickered across Emily's face, but she nodded. "Then let's move."

The guard, now appeased, waved them off, and Emily pushed the cart into the server room, her heart thudding with adrenaline and the rush of an unexpected ally at her side.

The server room hummed with the sound of powerful machines processing endless streams of data. Cool, sterile air prickled against Emily's skin as she set the box down on a metal table, eyes darting over the racks of servers. Mei moved with quiet precision, tapping a series of commands into a nearby console.

"Access codes are locked, but I can crack them," Mei whispered, her fingers flying over the keyboard. Emily kept an eye on the door, the tension coiled tightly in her chest.

"Lucas, I'm in," Emily said softly into her earpiece.

"Copy that," came Lucas's voice. She could almost hear the smile in his tone. "I've diverted security feeds, but you need to be quick. You've got five minutes before they do a systems check."

"Got it," Emily replied, her eyes meeting Mei's. The hacker nodded, glancing at her with a grin that hinted at mischief.

"Data extraction started," Mei said, pointing to a progress bar that slowly ticked forward on the screen.

A shadow crossed the room, and the sound of shoes squeaking on the floor sent a jolt through Emily's nerves. Before she could react, the towering figure of Wei Ling appeared in the doorway, his sharp gaze fixed on the girls.

"Well, well. Seems I have some uninvited guests," Ling drawled, his tone icy and commanding.

Emily's mind raced. "Sir, I was delivering these to IT. They said—"
Ling raised a hand to silence her, eyes narrowing. "Spare me the lies."

Lucas's voice crackled in her ear. "Emily, distraction incoming. Hold on."
The lights flickered, followed by a blaring alarm. Ling's expression shifted to irritation as he turned on his heel, barking orders into his phone. The momentary distraction was all Emily needed.

"You must go now!" Mei hissed, yanking the flash drive from the console and shoving it into Emily's hand.
She dashed down the hallway, footsteps echoing behind her. Emily's pulse pounded as she veered into a narrow maintenance corridor.

Lucas was waiting by a maintenance closet. He grabbed Emily's hand and pulled her inside. The space was cramped, their faces inches apart. His eyes searched hers, a silent question lingering between them. For a moment, the world outside fell away, replaced by the electricity crackling in the tight space.

"Lucas," Emily breathed, but before she could say more, footsteps pounded past the door. The danger snapped her back.

"Go," Lucas mouthed.

Emily nodded and slipped out, weaving through the narrow corridors of the building. Mei met her at the exit, eyes scanning their surroundings. "This way," she urged, guiding Emily to a side alley that led away from the building's bright lights.

The streets of Shanghai bustled with late-night energy—bright neon signs, laughter, and the hum of traffic.
Emily's pulse raced as she navigated the maze of alleys, sticking to shadows. She could hear the distant sound of sirens; someone must have triggered the alarm.

"We need to get you to the airport," Mei said, glancing over her shoulder. "But security will be tight."

Emily nodded, her mind already working through the next steps. They reached a main road, where Mei flagged down a motorized rickshaw. The driver, an older man with a kind face, didn't ask questions as they climbed in.

"Airport," Mei instructed, handing him a wad of bills.
The vehicle rattled and bumped down the street, the city lights blurring past. Emily's phone buzzed in her pocket. She pulled it out to see a message from Sophie.
Sophie: Just watched that new movie we planned to see. It wasn't the same without you. Miss you!
Emily's chest tightened with guilt. She quickly typed a reply.
Emily: Sorry, Soph. Can't wait to catch up. Promise we'll do something fun Monday.

The rickshaw pulled to a stop near the entrance to the airport. Mei turned to Emily, her expression serious. "Keep your head down and don't look back."
Emily squeezed Mei's hand. "Thank you. I owe you one."
Mei's eyes glimmered with a hint of a smile. "Stay safe, spy girl."

Chapter 5

The airport was a swirl of activity, and Emily's senses were on high alert. She weaved through the crowd, scanning for any sign of pursuit. Just as she reached the security checkpoint, a loud voice barked behind her.

"Stop! You, in the blue jacket!"
Emily's heart froze. She didn't dare turn around but kept moving forward, willing herself to stay calm. The security officer stepped past her, stopping another traveler. The rush of relief almost made her knees buckle.
She placed her bag on the conveyor belt, eyes darting nervously as it passed through the scanner. The uniformed officer at the machine peered at the screen, frowning slightly. Emily's breath caught, but then he waved her through with a curt nod.

Once she was past security, she exhaled shakily and headed to her gate. The boarding process was quick, and soon she was seated by the window, watching the city lights fade as the plane ascended into the sky.

——

The hum of the airplane engines was almost soothing. Emily pulled out her phone and checked for messages. There was one from her mom.

Mom: Hope your workshop is going well. Can't wait to hear all about it. Stay safe.

Emily's eyes stung with exhaustion and guilt.

Emily: Everything's good. Love you.

As the plane reached cruising altitude, her phone buzzed again. This time, it was an unknown number.

"Hey, Carter," came Lucas's voice, low and familiar.

Emily's heart skipped. "How did you get this number?" she whispered, glancing around to ensure no one could hear.

"I have my ways," he said, and she could hear the smirk in his tone. "Just wanted to make sure you made it out okay."

A small smile spread across her face. "I did. Barely."

Good," Lucas said, the line going quiet for a moment. "So, San Francisco, huh? That's quite the academic program."

Emily chuckled softly. "Yeah, they're intense."

"I bet. So, tell me something, Carter. When you're not dodging guards and cracking security systems, what do you do for fun?"

The question caught her off guard, warmth blooming in her chest. "Well, I'm not as exciting as you might think. I like reading, hanging out with my best friend, and watching bad movies."

"Bad movies?" Lucas sounded amused. "We might need to trade recommendations."
"Deal," Emily said, a genuine smile tugging at her lips. "And you? What's behind the mysterious agent act?"
Lucas's tone softened. "I like old cars and playing guitar when I get the chance. My family runs a small shop back home. I guess I'm not as mysterious as you thought."

The conversation drifted into a comfortable silence, the miles slipping by unnoticed. For the first time in a while, Emily felt a flicker of normalcy amidst the chaos.

"Get some rest, Carter," Lucas said finally. "You've earned it."

"You too," she whispered before the call ended, the steady drone of the engines lulling her into a light sleep as the plane soared towards home.

The plane descended smoothly, the golden hues of sunset casting a warm glow over the city below. Emily opened her eyes as the wheels touched down, the rumble of the tarmac vibrating through her seat. A deep breath steadied her nerves as she prepared for the final steps home.

The door of the plane opened, and a rush of cool evening air filled the cabin. Emily stepped out onto the tarmac, her hair whipping gently in the breeze.

Waiting for her was a sleek black sedan, its engine quietly purring. The driver, dressed impeccably in a dark suit, nodded as she approached.

"Welcome back, Miss Carter," he said, opening the rear door.
Emily slid into the car, the leather seats soft beneath her as she settled in. The city lights began to twinkle in the distance, mirroring the stars that dotted the darkening sky.

"Home," she murmured, leaning back as the car pulled away.

Her phone buzzed, and she glanced at the screen to see a message from Sophie.
Sophie: Sooo... are you back yet? I swear, you're more mysterious than a spy!

A smile touched Emily's lips.

Emily: I'm on my way home now. Can't wait to hear about your weekend... mine was SO boring!

The car sped through the quiet streets, and just as they passed the edge of the city, her phone pinged again—an incoming video call from Benson. She straightened, pushing the exhaustion from her face.

"Agent Carter," Benson's sharp features filled the screen. "Status report."

"Mission complete," Emily said, keeping her voice steady. "Data on Sentinel has been secured. Extraction went as planned."

"Good," Benson replied, eyes narrowing slightly. "Dupont, anything to add?"

Lucas's voice came through the call, calm and professional. "No additional details, sir. Everything proceeded smoothly."

Emily felt a slight twinge of tension—both she and Lucas had silently agreed to omit their close encounter and the phone call. It was better this way, she reasoned. Some moments were just theirs to keep.

Benson's gaze shifted between them. "Understood. You'll both receive further instructions soon. Carter, get some rest."

"Yes, sir," Emily said before the call ended.

The car pulled into her driveway just as the last traces of sunlight disappeared behind the horizon. Emily stepped out, breathing in the familiar scent of home. The porch light glowed softly, welcoming her back.

Inside, her mom was setting out bowls of freshly popped popcorn on the coffee table.

"Hey, sweetheart," her mom said, eyes lighting up. "Just in time for the Sunday movie."

Emily's dad appeared from the kitchen, a grin spreading across his face. "There she is! How was San Francisco?"

"Tiring," Emily admitted, sinking into the couch. "But I'm glad to be back."

Her mom handed her a bowl of popcorn, and Emily nestled between her parents, the warmth of home seeping into her tired limbs.

The familiar hum of the TV, the scent of buttered popcorn, and the quiet laughter of her family wrapped around her like a blanket, momentarily pushing away the weight of her double life.

Her phone buzzed again, and she glanced at it to find another message from Sophie.

Sophie: I have SO much to tell you! And don't even think about skipping out on tomorrow's hangout. I will drag you out of your house if I have to.

Emily's fingers danced over the keyboard.

Emily: Wouldn't dream of it. See you tomorrow.

She put her phone aside just as the movie started, allowing herself a rare moment of peace.

Later that evening, as the house quieted and her parents had drifted off to bed, her phone buzzed one last time. It was Lucas.

Lucas: Made it back okay?

Emily: Yeah, just in time for movie night with the fam.

Lucas: Good. You deserved a break. We'll talk soon.

Emily stared at the screen, a soft smile spreading across her face. The exhaustion of the mission still weighed on her, but for the first time in days, she felt a sense of balance—a sliver of normalcy amid the chaos.

Chapter 6

Monday morning came with the weight of exhaustion pressing down on Emily. The rhythmic sound of her alarm jolted her awake, and she rubbed her eyes, the remnants of her light sleep still clinging to her.

The glow of the sunrise spilled into her room, casting long shadows over her desk, cluttered with school books and notes hastily scrawled before she left for Shanghai.

She sighed, pulling herself out of bed and reminding herself that no matter how thrilling or dangerous her weekends were, Monday always brought her back to the mundane reality of high school.

The halls of Riverton High buzzed with the usual chatter. Emily walked past groups of students, their laughter and gossip blending into a background hum. She slipped into her first class, English, just as the bell rang. Sophie waved her over, eyebrows raised in a silent question. Emily mouthed "Later" as she slumped into her seat.

Halfway through the lesson, fatigue took over. Her eyelids grew heavy, and before she knew it, the classroom dissolved around her. She was back on the rooftops of Paris, the city lights glistening beneath her feet. Lucas stood beside her, a knowing smile playing at his lips.

"Stay focused, Carter," he said, his voice teasing.

"Emily!" Sophie's voice yanked her back to reality. Emily jolted awake to find Mr. Carson staring at her, arms crossed.

"Would you care to share your thoughts on Shakespeare's use of irony, Miss Carter?" he asked, the hint of a challenge in his voice.

Heat rushed to her cheeks. "Uh, it's—it's quite effective," she stammered, glancing at Sophie's suppressed giggle.

———

By Tuesday, Emily's energy had somewhat returned, but basketball practice was grueling.

The sound of sneakers squeaking on the polished wood, the shouts of her teammates, and Coach Parker's sharp whistle kept her grounded. Yet, even as she dribbled and passed, she caught Ryan's gaze more than once. He was leaning against the gym wall, his dark hair tousled and eyes twinkling with mischief.

"Nice pass, Carter," he called, giving her a grin.

Emily's heart sank—not with excitement, but with dread. Ryan was charming, that was undeniable, but the butterflies in her stomach refused to flutter for him. Not like they did for Lucas.

"Thanks," she muttered, shooting a three-pointer that clanged off the rim. Sophie, noticing the exchange, gave her a knowing look as they jogged down the court.

"He's been watching you all practice," Sophie whispered.

"Yeah, I noticed," Emily said, trying to sound casual. "Let's just say I have enough on my plate."

———

Wednesday and Thursday brought group projects in History, where they were tasked with presenting a report on Paris.

Emily's heart lurched when she saw the topic, memories of her last mission dancing just beneath the surface. Her group, consisting of Sophie, Ryan, and two other classmates, gathered in the library.

"So, Paris," Ryan said, leaning back in his chair. "Ever been, Emily? You seem like the type who'd have some cool stories."

Emily's fingers stilled on her notebook. "I've read a lot about it," she replied with a tight smile.

"You mean the Eiffel Tower and baguettes?" Sophie quipped, trying to steer the conversation away from Emily's growing discomfort.

"More than that," Emily added, suddenly inspired. "Like the hidden alleys with street art and the old cafes tucked away from the crowds."

Ryan's eyes lit up. "See? I knew you'd know the good stuff. We should all go sometime."

Emily's smile faltered for just a moment, and Sophie caught it, raising an eyebrow in silent concern.

———

Friday arrived with an electric anticipation buzzing through the halls.

The upcoming school dance was the talk of the day, students swapping plans and outfits with excited whispers. Emily walked to her locker, mentally preparing herself for the onslaught of chatter.

"Hey, Emily," Ryan said, appearing beside her. "So, are you going to the dance tonight?"
She forced a smile. "I don't think so. I have... family plans." The lie felt heavy on her tongue.
"Too bad," Ryan said, disappointment flashing across his face before he recovered. "Maybe next time."
Before Emily could respond, her phone buzzed in her pocket. A message from the agency.

New Mission Briefing. Report at 2100 hours.

The weight of her double life settled on her shoulders once more. As Ryan walked away, Sophie sidled up to her, eyes curious.

"Skipping the dance? You sure you're okay?"
Emily met Sophie's gaze, a mix of guilt and longing in her chest. "Yeah, I'm fine. Just... life, you know?"

Sophie sighed but nodded. "Well, don't let life pass you by too much, Em."

Emily's thoughts drifted back to Lucas, the thrill and confusion of their last mission replaying in her mind. The hall around her buzzed with teenage excitement, but her world felt split between the ordinary and the extraordinary.

And the distance between them was growing.

Chapter 7

Friday evening had settled over the Carter household, bringing with it a golden glow from the kitchen light and the soft clatter of dishes. Emily's parents stood by the doorway, her mom's hand resting on her dad's arm as they exchanged one last set of instructions.

"Now, Emily," her mom started, her tone laced with both concern and love. "We're trusting you to stay safe this weekend while we help Uncle Charlie move. No wild parties, no staying up too late, and keep the doors locked at all times."

Her dad chimed in with a half-smile. "And don't burn the house down trying to make those fancy grilled cheese sandwiches of yours."

Emily rolled her eyes but smiled back. "Yes, yes, I got it. Lock the doors, no late nights, no grilled cheese infernos. I'll be fine, I promise."

Her mom's eyes softened as she leaned in for a hug. "I know you will, sweetheart. But I had to say it."

"We'll be back Sunday night," her dad said, giving her a reassuring pat on the shoulder. "Call us if you need anything."

"Will do," Emily replied, watching them step out into the driveway, the glow of the car headlights briefly illuminating the living room before fading as they pulled away.

With a sigh, she turned back to the kitchen, eyeing the remnants of dinner—spaghetti sauce splatters, a half-empty salad bowl, and plates stacked precariously in the sink. Might as well get this over with, she thought, rolling up her sleeves.

The house was finally quiet as Emily finished the last dish and wiped her hands on a towel. She plopped down on the couch, sinking into the cushions and letting out a long breath. The hum of the TV filled the background, playing some late-night comedy show she wasn't paying attention to. Just as her eyes began to close, the screen flickered and went black.

Emily bolted upright, her heart thudding as the screen brightened again—but this time, Benson's stern face appeared, filling the TV.

"Agent Carter," his voice crackled through the room.
"Benson," Emily said, swallowing the surprise. "You're on my TV now? That's... new."

"Urgent times call for unconventional methods," Benson replied, his eyes narrowing. "We have a situation."
Emily straightened, the exhaustion of the day evaporating in an instant. "What's the mission?"

"You're heading to Iceland. A rogue scientist, Dr. Magnus Kristoff, has been working on a formula to create super-soldiers. Intelligence reports indicate he's close to perfecting it. Your objective is to infiltrate his lab and extract the formula before it's too late."
Emily's pulse quickened at the gravity of the mission. "Understood. When do I leave?"
"In one hour. Your transport will be waiting at the usual pickup point," Benson said. He paused, a rare flicker of hesitation crossing his face. "There's one more thing. Due to the high stakes, we're assigning a partner to assist you."
Emily's heart stopped. "A partner?"
The screen shifted slightly, and another familiar face appeared beside Benson—Lucas. His blue eyes met hers with a spark of amusement.
"Hope you're ready for the cold, Carter," Lucas said, the corner of his mouth lifting in a grin.
Emily's breath caught in her chest.

She forced herself to nod, trying to keep her expression neutral despite the warmth spreading through her. "Always am, Dupont."

Benson's voice interrupted the moment. "You two will be briefed in detail on the plane. Make no mistake—this is a high-risk operation. Stay sharp."
"Understood," Emily said, her voice steady.

The screen blinked off, leaving the room bathed in silence once more. Emily sat for a moment, the adrenaline humming beneath her skin. She glanced around the empty room, the normalcy of it all feeling surreal compared to the task ahead.

She stood up, grabbing her go-bag from the hall closet and mentally running through her checklist. The chill of Iceland wouldn't be the only thing testing her limits this weekend—Lucas's presence added a new layer of complication she hadn't anticipated.
But there was no time to dwell. This mission wouldn't wait, and neither would she.

——

The ride to the pickup point was swift and silent, the streets dark and empty. The private jet sat on the tarmac, its sleek silhouette glowing under the runway lights.

As she stepped on board, the warmth of the cabin wrapped around her, and she spotted Lucas lounging in a seat, a confident smirk on his face.

"Welcome aboard," he said, his voice low.

Emily raised an eyebrow, the corner of her mouth lifting. Just then, the monitor mounted on the wall lit up, and Benson's face appeared once more. The hum of the jet engines idled as he began the briefing.

"Agents, your target, Dr. Kristoff, operates out of a fortified facility beneath a glacier. The lab is protected by advanced surveillance and a team of trained mercenaries. You'll need to disable the security grid before entering the main lab. The formula itself is stored in a secure vault, accessed only with biometric data."

Lucas's eyes met Emily's, the tension palpable.

"Your insertion point will be here," Benson continued, pointing to a digital map showing an isolated stretch of ice. "Expect temperatures well below freezing, so prepare accordingly. Once inside, extraction will be tight. An alarm will trigger a lockdown with reinforcements arriving within ten minutes."

"Sounds cozy," Lucas muttered under his breath, earning a half-smile from Emily.

Benson's eyes narrowed as if he had heard. "Keep your wits about you. Failure is not an option."

"Understood," they both replied in unison. The screen flickered off, leaving them with the gentle hum of the engines.

Lucas shifted in his seat, turning to Emily. "So, what's your plan for staying warm out there?"

Emily leaned back, a small laugh escaping her lips. "Layer up and hope for the best. And you?"

"I'm more of a 'complain about it until it's over' kind of guy," Lucas said, grinning.

Emily couldn't help but chuckle, the tension in her chest easing slightly. She studied him as he talked, noting the way his eyes sparkled when he joked. Despite the danger and the stakes, there was a comfort in having him beside her. It was unsettling and reassuring all at once.

"You know, for someone who acts so nonchalant, you're pretty good at this spy stuff," Emily teased.

"Ah, my secret's out," Lucas said, leaning in conspiratorially. "It's all an act. I'm actually terrified most of the time."

"Right," Emily said, rolling her eyes, but the smile stayed on her face.

After a few more exchanges, Emily excused herself to change into her pajamas. The narrow bathroom was dimly lit, and she splashed cold water on her face to steady herself. When she stepped out, tugging at the hem of her sweatshirt, her eyes widened at the sight before her.

Lucas was in the process of changing, his shirt off and revealing a well-toned chest. He glanced up, his own expression caught between surprise and a hint of embarrassment.

"Oh, sorry," Emily stammered.
Lucas smiled in a way that made her heart skip a beat.

Chapter 8

Emily's cheeks flushed, but she wasn't really sorry. Lucas's eyes met hers, a twinkle of amusement and something warmer reflected in them as he paused, shirt half-draped in his hands. The silence between them stretched, charged with unspoken words

"Didn't mean to interrupt," Emily said, her voice catching slightly as she tried to play it cool.

"No worries," Lucas said, slipping the shirt over his head with a grin that made her heart stutter. "I guess we're past first impressions, aren't we?"

Emily laughed, the sound breaking the tension and settling them back into an easy camaraderie. "Yeah, I'd say so. If infiltrating enemy bases together doesn't do it, nothing will."

Emily noticed his eyes looking at every inch of her. Her heart was beating so fast!

Lucas's eyes softened as he sat on the edge of one of the bunks. "Speaking of which," he nodded toward the room, "we might need to have a talk about sleeping arrangements. This isn't exactly the five-star setup."

Emily's eyes followed his gaze, landing on the top bunk with its lopsided tilt and broken frame. The bottom bunk looked stable enough, but it was clear there was only one.

"Looks like someone's taking the recliner," she joked, gesturing to the single leather chair bolted into the corner of the cabin.

Lucas chuckled, but there was a touch of reluctance behind it. "I'll take it," he said, standing up with an exaggerated sigh. "You take the bed. Can't have you losing sleep before tomorrow's mission."

Emily opened her mouth to argue but hesitated, noticing the fleeting shadow in his eyes. He didn't really want to take the recliner, she could tell. And, truth be told, she didn't want him to, either.

"Are you sure?" she asked, more softly this time. The playful smile dropped from Lucas's face, replaced by something more serious. He looked at her for a moment longer, as if trying to read her mind.

"Yeah, I'm sure," he said, his voice low. "I've had worse nights."

But as Lucas settled into the recliner, shifting uncomfortably and folding his arms across his chest, Emily felt a pang of guilt mixed with a strange, fluttering warmth. She pulled the thin blanket over herself, listening to the quiet hum of the jet engines as they sped through the night. Sleep came in fits and starts. Every time Emily shifted, she found herself peeking at Lucas, who seemed to be in a restless half-sleep, eyes flickering open now and then. When he finally caught her staring for the third time, he smirked.

"Something on your mind?" he whispered.
Emily grinned, turning her head to the side. "Just making sure our top agent is still with us."
"Right," Lucas muttered, tilting his head back with a sigh. "Don't worry about me. Get some rest, Carter."

It wasn't long after that she drifted off, lulled by the steady beat of the engines and the warmth of the cabin.

She was only vaguely aware of the way Lucas's breathing had evened out, matching hers in the dim light.

The jolt of the plane's descent woke them both. Emily's eyes snapped open as she felt the familiar pressure shift in her ears. Lucas was already moving, straightening up with a groan as he stretched his arms above his head.

"Looks like we're here," he said, his voice raspy with sleep. Emily rubbed her eyes, the reality of the mission settling back over her like a heavy cloak. "Time to get to work," she muttered, throwing off the blanket and sitting up.

Lucas's eyes caught hers for a brief moment, and a small smile curved his lips. "Stay sharp, Carter."

She nodded, the warmth of the night's shared silence lingering for just a second longer before they both turned to the task ahead. The cold, unforgiving landscape of Iceland awaited, and with it, all the danger they'd been preparing for.

———

The icy wind whipped across Emily's face the moment she stepped off the jet, biting through her layered clothing and sending a shiver down her spine. The sky was an endless stretch of dark grey, tinged with hints of morning light.

Snow crunched beneath her boots as she surveyed the desolate landscape. Lucas fell into step beside her, his face set in determined lines.

Remember the insertion point," he said, adjusting the strap of his gear bag. His breath clouded in the freezing air. "We have to stay low until we reach the ridge."

"Got it," Emily replied, her voice muffled by the scarf wrapped around her mouth. The sound of the jet engines faded behind them, swallowed by the howling wind as they made their way toward the craggy expanse of ice and rock. Every step was a battle against the elements. The snowdrifts were knee-deep, and the slope ahead promised a grueling climb. Emily's muscles burned with exertion, but she pushed forward, matching Lucas's pace. The ridge loomed above them, jagged and daunting. They reached it with labored breaths, ducking behind a formation of ice to catch their breath.

"Look," Lucas whispered, nodding toward the faint glow of lights below. A cluster of steel structures, stark against the white expanse, marked Dr. Kristoff's facility.

Emily scanned the compound, her eyes narrowing. "Surveillance drones," she noted, pointing at the small, dark shapes patrolling the perimeter.

"And guards. Armed to the teeth," Lucas added grimly. "This is going to be tricky."

They shared a look, the weight of the mission pressing down on them. There was no room for mistakes. Emily took a deep breath and unfastened the grappling hook from her belt.

"Ready?" she asked.

Lucas smirked, his blue eyes glinting. "Always."

The hook shot up and caught on the ledge above. Emily tested it before swinging herself up and over, landing silently on the other side. Lucas followed, his movements practiced and fluid. They crept toward the nearest building, sticking to the shadows as the icy wind stung their faces.

Suddenly, the sound of footsteps crunched in the snow behind them. Emily's pulse quickened as she pressed herself against the cold metal of the wall. A guard rounded the corner, his flashlight slicing through the dark. Emily held her breath, the pounding of her heart loud in her ears.

"Stay still," Lucas whispered, barely audible.

The guard paused, the beam of light sweeping inches from their feet. Emily's fingers tightened around the handle of her knife, ready for action.

But after an agonizing moment, the guard muttered something in Icelandic and continued his patrol. Emily exhaled slowly.

"Too close," she said, exchanging a tense glance with Lucas.

"Let's move," he replied.

They skirted the edge of the compound, making their way to a side door marked with the symbol for restricted access. Emily pulled out her lock-picking tools, fingers numb as she worked. The tumblers clicked into place, and the door swung open with a soft groan.

Inside, the air was marginally warmer, smelling of metal and cold electricity. The hallways were dimly lit, the hum of generators thrumming beneath their feet.

"Control room is down this way," Lucas whispered, nodding toward a corridor to their right.

They moved swiftly, the silence broken only by the faint clatter of boots on metal grates. Suddenly, a red light flared, and an alarm blared through the facility. Emily's stomach dropped.

"They know we're here," Lucas said, his voice sharp. "Go! We have to get to the data before they lock it down."

Emily sprinted ahead, her mind racing.

They burst into the control room, startling a technician who fumbled for the emergency button. Lucas moved in a blur, subduing him with a swift strike.

"Cover me," Emily said, sliding into the chair and hacking into the mainframe. Her fingers flew across the keyboard, the code flashing on the screen as she bypassed security protocols. Sweat beaded on her forehead despite the chill.

"Hurry, Emily," Lucas said, positioning himself at the door with his gun raised as shouts and pounding footsteps echoed closer.

"Almost there," she muttered. The file appeared, and she transferred it onto the drive just as the first guards appeared.

Lucas fired a warning shot, and the guards hesitated, ducking behind the doorway. "Time's up!" he shouted. Emily yanked the drive from the terminal and nodded. "Let's go!"

They raced down the hallway, alarms still wailing. A blast of cold air hit them as they exited the building, the distant whir of drones closing in.
"Snowmobiles," Lucas said, spotting two parked by the perimeter.

"Perfect," Emily said, vaulting onto one and starting the engine. The roar drowned out the sound of her heartbeat as they sped into the icy expanse, the lights of the compound shrinking behind them.

A shot pinged off the metal frame of her snowmobile, and she glanced back to see guards taking aim. Lucas pulled up beside her, his eyes fierce.

"Keep going!" he yelled.
They maneuvered through the rough terrain, the wind biting at their exposed skin. The pounding of their pursuers faded as the landscape swallowed them whole. Only then did Emily allow herself a breath, the adrenaline still coursing through her veins.
"We did it," she said, her voice barely audible over the wind.
Lucas met her gaze, a rare smile breaking through the tension. "Yeah, we did."
But Emily knew it wasn't over yet. The real challenge was surviving long enough to make it back.

They reached the extraction point just as the faintest sliver of dawn began to lighten the horizon. The jet waited, engines rumbling and warm air spilling from its open door. Emily's limbs felt like lead as she clambered aboard, Lucas close behind.

"Welcome back," the pilot said, nodding as they collapsed into the cabin.

Emily slumped into a seat, the heat of the jet enveloping her in a blanket of relief. Lucas sat across from her, their eyes meeting in a moment of silent triumph. But before exhaustion could claim them, he stood and walked over, glancing at the single bunk.

"Looks like it's still busted," he said, the corner of his mouth twitching.

Emily laughed softly, the sound breaking the tension. "Guess we'll have to share."

Lucas's eyes held hers, the unspoken agreement sparking between them. "If you're okay with it," he said, his voice low.

"I am," Emily replied, shifting to make space.

Chapter 9

They lay down, the narrow bunk pressing them close. The warmth of his body seeped into hers, and she felt his arm slide around her waist, tentative at first. She turned to face him, their noses almost touching. The jet hummed around them, a comforting backdrop.

"We made it," Lucas whispered, brushing a strand of hair from her face.

"Yeah," she said, her breath mingling with his. Their eyes locked, and the space between them disappeared as their lips met, tentative and searching at first before deepening with a shared sense of victory and relief. His hand trailed up her back, sending shivers that had nothing to do with the cold.

Emily pulled back slightly, a smile curving her lips. "You know, this isn't exactly protocol."

They settled into a comfortable silence, the tension of the mission melting away as sleep finally claimed them.

The sudden jolt of the landing gear woke them, and Emily blinked against the light streaming through the window. Lucas stirred beside her, their limbs tangled in the cramped space.

"Time to wake up beautiful," he said, voice rough with sleep but eyes alert.

Emily's eyelids fluttered open, and a smile curved her lips as she met his gaze. The reality of the mission's success and the safety of their return flooded her with relief. Lucas's hand lingered at her waist, their closeness a tangible reminder of the night's shared moments. Without a second thought, she leaned in, capturing his lips in a slow, tender kiss. It was gentle yet laced with the unspoken gratitude and exhilaration of having survived together.

"We should get ready," she whispered against his mouth, their breath mingling as they lingered in the fleeting quiet. "Yeah," Lucas agreed, though neither of them moved for a long, shared heartbeat.

The plane touched down smoothly, and the cabin crew opened the door to let the crisp evening air sweep in. Lucas and Emily exchanged knowing glances as they gathered their gear. By the time they descended the steps and made their way to the waiting car, the sun was starting to set, bathing the tarmac in pale gold.

Lucas opened the car door for Emily and right before she was about to get in, he gently turned her face and brought his lips down to meet hers. Their eyes locked in silence and a knowing smile.

The car ride to the debriefing location was subdued, the adrenaline of the mission still pulsing through them. Benson's voice on speaker punctuated the silence.

"Agent Carter, we will drop you off first. Further analysis and documentation will follow in your reports. Rest assured, this has been a commendable effort on both your parts. Agent Dupont, you will proceed to HQ for an additional briefing."

Emily's chest tightened at the thought of saying goodbye, even temporarily. She kept her face composed, nodding at Benson's orders.

"Understood, sir," she said, her voice steady, betraying nothing.

The car pulled up to her street, the familiar sight of her neighborhood just beginning to stir in the early morning light. Lucas reached out, fingers brushing hers as they exchanged a look that spoke volumes—gratitude, longing, and the unspoken promise of more.

"Be safe, Emily," he said, his voice low but firm.

"You too," she replied, a tight smile playing on her lips as she resisted the urge to lean into him one last time.

She pushed the door open, the cool air hitting her as she stepped out. Before closing it, she turned back, meeting Lucas's eyes.

"See you soon," she added, her voice carrying a subtle weight.

He nodded, the corners of his mouth lifting ever so slightly. The car pulled away, and Emily watched it disappear down the street, the warmth of their parting touch lingering in the cool evening.

With a deep breath, she turned and walked up the steps to her house, the familiar creak of the porch floorboards underfoot grounding her. The key turned smoothly in the lock, and she slipped inside, dropping her bag by the door. The house was quiet, holding that serene stillness that comes just before life rushes back in.

She glanced at the clock on the wall—just enough time to compose herself before her parents returned.

The mission's tension ebbed away, replaced by the soft hum of anticipation for their arrival and the normalcy it promised.

Emily sank into the couch, letting her head fall back with a sigh. The memory of Lucas's touch and the echo of his words played through her mind. In that moment, she felt both the weight of her double life and the rare, fleeting warmth that made it all worthwhile.

A sudden pang of guilt tugged at her as she realized she hadn't heard from Sophie all weekend. Sophie, her best friend who'd been through thick and thin with her, deserved better. Without hesitation, Emily grabbed her phone and dialed Sophie's number.

The call connected, and Sophie's voice, tired and edged with frustration, answered. "Hey, Em."
"Hey, Soph. I'm sorry I didn't reach out this weekend," Emily began, her voice faltering. "Things were... complicated."

There was a pause, and then Sophie's sigh crackled through the line. "Complicated. Right. It's always complicated with you, isn't it? Emily, I'm tired of the half-truths and disappearing acts. I know there's more going on than you're telling me."

Emily's heart sank, guilt twisting like a knife in her chest. "Sophie, I—"

"No, Em. You don't get to brush this off with another vague excuse," Sophie interrupted, her voice breaking. "I feel like I'm losing my best friend, and I don't even know why."

Emily swallowed hard, tears pricking at the corners of her eyes. "You're not losing me. I promise you're not. Meet me tomorrow morning before school. I'll tell you everything."

The line was silent for a moment, and Emily could almost hear Sophie's breath hitch. "You mean it?" Sophie whispered.

"I do," Emily said, her voice steady now. "No more secrets."

"Okay," Sophie replied, a mixture of hope and wariness in her tone. "Tomorrow."

"Tomorrow," Emily echoed, letting out a breath she hadn't realized she was holding.

Just then, the sound of car doors slamming shut outside made her heart leap. She quickly wiped her eyes as her parents walked up the driveway. The front door opened, and her mom's warm voice filled the entryway.

"Emily? We're home!"

"Hey, Mom! Dad!" Emily called, forcing a smile as they stepped into the living room, their faces lighting up when they saw her.

"How was your weekend, sweetie?" her dad asked, dropping his bags and giving her a hug.

"Pretty quiet," Emily said, hugging him back tightly, the familiar scent of home washing over her. "I'm glad you're back."
"We missed you," her mom added, brushing a stray hair from Emily's face. "Anything exciting happen?"

Emily's heart thudded, but she kept her smile in place. "Just the usual."

As her parents moved to unpack, Emily glanced out the window, the weight of tomorrow's promise heavy on her shoulders. For the first time, the thought of revealing her secret felt less like an end and more like the beginning of something truer.

Chapter 10

Monday dawned with a crisp chill in the air, the last remnants of dawn's golden glow settling over the small park beside the school. Emily sat on the cold bench, hands shoved deep into the pockets of her jacket, her breath visible in the morning air. She'd been rehearsing this conversation all weekend, but now that it was moments away, her pulse thudded erratically in her chest.

The rustle of leaves drew her attention, and Sophie appeared on the path, her expression a mix of confusion and worry. She slowed as she approached, eyes narrowing as she studied Emily's tense posture.

"Hey," Sophie said cautiously, sitting beside her but leaving a small gap between them.

"Hey," Sophie said cautiously, sitting beside her but leaving a small gap between them.

"Hey," Emily replied, offering a small, strained smile. Silence hung between them for a moment, punctuated only by the distant sounds of cars and the laughter of younger kids playing in the distance.

"So," Sophie finally broke the silence, crossing her arms and leaning forward. "You said you'd tell me everything. No more secrets, remember?"

Emily nodded, drawing in a deep breath. "I meant it," she said, her voice barely above a whisper. "Sophie, there's a reason I've been... distant, and why I'm always running off or too tired to think straight. It's not what you think. It's bigger."

Sophie's brows knitted together, her concern shifting to a guarded skepticism. "Bigger than your parents grounding you for sneaking out? Bigger than school stuff?"

Emily met Sophie's eyes, searching for the understanding she hoped to find. "I'm a spy," she said, the words hanging in the cold morning air like an impossibility.

Sophie's eyes widened, her mouth parting as if to laugh, but the look on Emily's face stopped her. "Wait... what? Are you joking?"

"I wish I were," Emily said, a bitter edge to her voice. "It started a year ago, when my parents and I went on that adventure vacation. Remember the paintball competition?"

Sophie's gaze flicked downward as she tried to piece it together. "Yeah, you won that tournament against all those adults. You said it was the best weekend ever."

"It was, until I caught the attention of a few people who weren't just spectators," Emily continued, the memories rushing back—the exhilaration of outmaneuvering grown men, the sharp, analytical eyes that had followed her from the sidelines. "The agency approached me after the trip. They said I had a natural talent—situational awareness, strategy, and precision. At first, I thought it was some kind of prank."

Sophie's face shifted from disbelief to shock, her eyes searching Emily's for any sign of a lie. "And you said yes? Just like that?"

"Not immediately," Emily admitted, twisting her fingers in her lap. "It took weeks of convincing and secret meetings. They said they needed someone young, someone who could blend in. And Sophie, it's not just fieldwork. I've trained for this—hard."

Sophie sat back, her expression stunned into silence. When she finally spoke, her voice was shaky. "So, all those times you canceled plans, all those excuses—they were real?"

Emily nodded, eyes glistening with unshed tears. "I wanted to tell you so many times, but I couldn't. It's classified, and if anything happened to you because of me..." She let the sentence trail off, the weight of it pressing between them.

Sophie's eyes softened, confusion giving way to an overwhelming mixture of relief and betrayal. "Emily, I don't know what to say. I thought you didn't trust me, that you were just... done with me."
"Never," Emily whispered, reaching out to take Sophie's hand. "You're my best friend. You deserve the truth, even if it's dangerous."

The morning bell rang in the distance, jolting them back to reality. Sophie's eyes darted to the school, then back to Emily. "This changes everything," she said, a small, incredulous smile breaking through. "But at least now I know."
Emily nodded, squeezing Sophie's hand. "Yeah. Now you know."

———

The rest of the day at school was a blur.

Emily's teachers seemed more observant than usual, their eyes lingering on her when she stifled yawns or when her gaze drifted out the window. The principal even passed by her class, glancing in with a suspicious frown.

"Ms. Carter, are we boring you?" Mr. Allen's voice snapped her back to the present. The entire class turned to stare, some with amused smiles, others with raised eyebrows.

"No, sir," Emily said quickly, straightening in her seat. "Just... didn't sleep well last night."

"Is that so?" Mr. Allen said, the skepticism clear in his voice. "Try to keep your focus, please."

"Yes, Mr. Allen," she replied, suppressing an eye roll.

As the day dragged on, Emily found herself weaving increasingly creative excuses. To Sophie's credit, she played along during lunch when Emily launched into a ridiculous story about a raccoon sneaking into her yard and keeping her up all night.

"A raccoon? Really?" one of their classmates, Maya, asked, eyes wide with skepticism.

"Oh, you have no idea," Sophie chimed in with a smirk, "It was practically doing gymnastics."

Emily shot her a grateful look, a flicker of humor sparking between them despite the tension.

But underneath it all, the risk of exposure loomed larger than ever.

——

As the final bell rang and students filtered out of the classrooms, Emily felt her phone buzz in her pocket. She pulled it out discreetly and glanced at the screen. Her blood ran cold.

Lucas: 911. HELP.

A wave of panic surged through her, tightening her chest and making her palms clammy. Her mind raced, scenarios and worst-case outcomes flashing through her head like lightning.

"Emily?" Sophie's voice cut through the noise, pulling her back. Sophie's eyes searched hers with concern. "What's wrong?"

Emily swallowed hard, trying to keep her voice steady. "Uh, I just got a text—family emergency," she said, forcing a smile that felt brittle. "I need to go."

Sophie's eyes narrowed slightly, as if sensing the strain beneath Emily's calm. "Want me to come with you?"

"No," Emily said, a bit too quickly. She took a breath and softened her tone. "Thanks, but I'll be fine. Just... cover for me, okay?"

Before Sophie could respond, another vibration in Emily's pocket made her heart stop. This time, it was an alert from the agency's emergency communication app.

Agent Carter: Immediate assistance required. An agent is in jeopardy. Details classified.
Her breath caught in her throat, but deep down, she knew. It was Lucas.

"Sophie, I really need to go," Emily said, grabbing her bag and moving with an urgency that couldn't be disguised. "Please, just trust me."

Chapter 11

Sophie's eyes followed her, concern warring with confusion. "Be safe, Emily," she called after her.

Emily pushed through the crowded hallways, weaving around chattering students and teachers who barely glanced her way. The noise of lockers slamming and footsteps pounding the linoleum floor buzzed around her, but it all felt muted—a distant hum beneath the storm inside her. Her heart thudded with urgency as she slipped into an empty classroom and locked the door behind her.
She took a deep breath, fingers trembling as she tapped out a series of commands on her phone to activate a secure line. The screen glowed with the agency's emblem before Benson's familiar, steely face appeared.

"Agent Carter, you received the alert," Benson said without preamble. His eyes, cold and calculating, scanned her face for any sign of hesitation.

"Yes, sir. What's the situation?" Emily's voice was steady, but the tightness in her chest refused to loosen. Her mind was already several steps ahead, trying to piece together the fragments of information.

Benson's face softened, just for a moment—an unusual slip. "An extraction mission in Prague has gone sideways. Agent Dupont's cover was compromised during an intel exchange. He's currently evading pursuit but has limited resources. Your task is to intercept and assist in the extraction."

Emily's heart clenched. Lucas. The name echoed in her mind like a drumbeat. She felt a rush of panic that threatened to bubble over but forced herself to remain calm.

"Understood. Do we have a location?"

Benson nodded, the connection crackling slightly as he transmitted coordinates to her device. "He's near the Old Town Square, moving toward the Charles Bridge. The enemy's operatives are highly trained and heavily armed. This will not be easy, Agent Carter."

Emily's jaw set. "I'll manage. What's my exit strategy?"

"Local safe house near the west bank. Full extraction details will be provided upon successful contact," Benson replied. His eyes narrowed as if searching for any sign of doubt in her expression. "Are you ready for this?"
Emily took a deep breath, the weight of unspoken emotions pressing down on her. "Yes, sir. I'll bring him home."

The screen blinked out, leaving her in the dim light of the classroom. She stood still for a moment, letting the tension pulse through her veins. Thoughts of Lucas swirled in her mind—his confident smirk, the way he'd called her "beautiful" in that teasing tone, the spark in his eyes when he glanced her way. It wasn't just the mission. It was him. The fear of losing him gnawed at her, sharper than any training she'd ever endured.

The loud ring of her phone snapped her back into focus. She glanced down at the notification: her parents' number. Guilt surged through her, but she quickly sent a message explaining she had to stay late for a group project and would be home later.
With the excuse sent and her bag packed, Emily slipped out of the classroom and out the side door of the school. The chilly breeze nipped at her face as she raced down the block, away from prying eyes, toward her rendezvous point.

The sleek, black SUV idled in an alley, engine purring like a caged animal. Emily yanked open the passenger door and climbed in, her pulse still hammering. The driver, another field agent she recognized as Greer, shot her a quick nod.

"Got the details?" Greer asked, voice clipped.

"Yes. Let's move," Emily said, fastening her seatbelt. The vehicle roared to life, speeding through the maze of city streets toward the private airstrip. The tension in the car was suffocating, each second stretching into eternity.

As the city blurred by, Emily's thoughts drifted to Lucas again. She could almost see him, ducking through narrow alleys with that fierce determination she knew so well. The thought of him alone and cornered sent a shiver down her spine. She squeezed her eyes shut, willing herself to keep it together. He needed her, and she would not fail him.

"We'll get him out," Greer said, as if reading her mind. His eyes met hers in the rearview mirror, offering a rare moment of reassurance.

Emily nodded, determination hardening her features. "We have to."

As they sped toward the airport, Emily pulled out her phone and typed a quick message to Sophie:

Emily: Sophie, I need a huge favor. Can you tell my parents I'm staying over at your place tonight to work on the group project? Long story, but I'll explain later.

Seconds ticked by before Sophie's reply appeared on her screen.

Sophie: Are you serious? This is more of that spy stuff, isn't it?

Emily: Yes, but I'll be safe. Please, Soph. Just this once.

A pause, then Sophie replied:

Sophie: Fine, but you owe me a full explanation. And you better be safe, or I'm telling your parents everything.

Emily: I promise. Thank you!

Emily's phone buzzed almost immediately with a text from her mom:

Mom: Sophie just called. Be safe and behave! I want you home right after school tomorrow.

Relief washed over Emily as she quickly replied, thanking her mom for understanding.

The SUV pulled up to the private airstrip, and Emily quickly boarded the sleek jet. As she strapped in, the engines roared to life, and they took off into the sky. The city lights faded beneath them, replaced by the vast darkness of the night.

Sitting back, Emily forced herself to breathe, focusing on the mission ahead. Lucas was out there, and he was counting on her. The thought of him, alone and in danger, filled her with equal parts dread and determination.

Her fingers traced the edge of her phone, heart pounding as she replayed his last text. She couldn't fail him.

The captain's voice crackled over the intercom. "Agent Carter, we'll be landing in approximately twenty minutes."

Emily tightened her grip on the armrest, her mind steeling for whatever lay ahead. The city lights of Prague glimmered below as the jet began its descent.

Chapter 12

The jet touched down in the outskirts of Prague, its wheels skimming over the tarmac as Emily took a deep, steadying breath. No sooner had the plane come to a halt than she grabbed her gear, exiting to meet the agency team waiting on the ground.

Agent Greer was already coordinating. "Alright, Agent Carter," he said, motioning her over to a map displayed on a tablet. "Dupont's last known location was here, near the Old Town Square. He's moving east, likely toward the Charles Bridge, evading multiple hostiles. Our team is intercepting the operatives in pairs to narrow down their range."
Emily nodded, adrenaline sharp in her veins. "I need to get closer. Any details on the hostiles?"

Greer shook his head. "We've only confirmed two identities—both are high-ranking. Armed and highly skilled."

"Then let's get moving," Emily replied, slipping her earpiece in.

Greer nodded, signaling to the other agents. They moved swiftly, breaking off in small teams as they disappeared into the maze of historic streets, their shadows blending into the city's darkness.

Emily kept her focus sharp, her footsteps light as she navigated the winding alleys. The familiar hum of her earpiece activated. "Carter, I'm linking you to Dupont's channel," Greer's voice came through. "He's close by."

A faint, muffled sound followed—a voice she'd recognize anywhere.

"Emily…" Lucas's voice was strained, barely above a whisper. "Got… pinned near the bridge… three operatives… northwest side."

Her heart clenched, but she forced herself to stay calm. "Hold on, Lucas. I'm almost there. Just keep talking so I can find you."

Emily's eyes scanned her surroundings, the darkened buildings casting long, looming shadows.

Then, a sudden flash—a glint of metal from around a corner up ahead. She slowed her steps, pressing herself against the wall, inching closer. Her voice remained low but steady. "Lucas, I see them. I'm going to create a distraction, but when you get an opening, move south. Got it?"

"Understood," he replied, a hint of relief threading through the exhaustion in his voice.

Emily drew a small device from her pocket, a flash charge. She tossed it into the alley ahead, ducking as it erupted in a brilliant burst of light, illuminating the narrow space. She heard the startled shouts of the operatives and took her chance, slipping in close enough to see Lucas huddled behind a stone barricade, his face pale but determined.

"Now, Lucas!" she hissed, motioning to him.

He shot up from his hiding spot, dodging one of the operatives who lunged toward him. Emily blocked the operative's path, sweeping her leg to knock him off balance, then grabbing Lucas's arm and pulling him along with her down a side alley.

"Left up ahead!" she instructed, leading him through a series of narrow passages that twisted deeper into the heart of the city.

The sounds of their pursuers grew fainter, but Emily didn't stop until they reached a small, deserted square tucked in between the towering buildings.

Then, a sudden flash—a glint of metal from around a corner up ahead. She slowed her steps, pressing herself against the wall, inching closer. Her voice remained low but steady. "Lucas, I see them. I'm going to create a distraction, but when you get an opening, move south. Got it?"

"Understood," he replied, a hint of relief threading through the exhaustion in his voice.

"Left up ahead!" she instructed, leading him through a series of narrow passages that twisted deeper into the heart of the city.

The sounds of their pursuers grew fainter, but Emily didn't stop until they reached a small, deserted square tucked between the towering buildings.

Lucas slumped against a wall, his breathing ragged. Emily placed a hand on his shoulder, her eyes scanning him with concern. "Are you okay?"

He nodded, his usual grin returning. "Nothing a night in a five-star hotel wouldn't fix."

Emily rolled her eyes, but a smile tugged at her lips. "Not exactly agency protocol."

They shared a laugh, their relief palpable in the quiet square. The adrenaline of the chase gave way to a softer silence as they both caught their breath.

Lucas broke it first, his gaze holding hers. "I thought I was done for," he admitted, his tone dropping to a vulnerability she rarely heard from him.

Emily's heart skipped as she took a step closer. "Not on my watch," she whispered, her hand lingering on his arm. The intensity of the moment settled between them, her pulse quickening as he leaned in slightly, their faces mere inches apart.

"Thank you, Emily," he murmured, his voice barely above a breath.

Her hand moved up to his cheek, her thumb brushing lightly against his skin. "I couldn't let anything happen to you."

Their eyes met, an unspoken understanding passing between them, and, for a brief moment, the world faded away as they shared a soft, lingering kiss. It was tentative yet filled with the emotion they'd both held back for so long.

They pulled back slowly, Lucas's eyes holding a mischievous glint. "You know, we really should get back to base, or we'll miss the plane."
Emily smirked, her hand slipping from his cheek. "I suppose you're right. Can't have you playing the hero without me."
The jet's engines hummed steadily as they flew through the night sky, the city of Prague shrinking beneath them. Lucas sat beside her, the tension from the mission replaced by a comfortable silence.

After a few minutes, Lucas leaned in, his eyes sparkling with something playful. "By the way, I have a surprise for you this weekend." Emily raised an eyebrow, curiosity sparking in her eyes. "A surprise? Are you going to give me a hint at least? Something small?"

Lucas leaned casually against the wall, his grin widening. "Not a chance. But I promise, you'll love it."

Emily crossed her arms, pretending to look unimpressed. "Oh, come on, Lucas. Is it something dangerous? Because if it is, I'm out."
He chuckled, shaking his head. "Dangerous? No way. Well... not unless you count having too much fun as dangerous."
Emily tilted her head, studying him. "Too much fun? You're not exactly filling me with confidence here. Is this one of your wild ideas again?"""

Lucas raised his hands in mock defense. "Wild? Me? Emily, you wound me. Just trust me on this one, okay?"

She sighed dramatically but couldn't hide the small smile tugging at her lips. "Fine. But if I end up covered in glitter or something, you're paying for the dry cleaning."

"Noted," Lucas said with a laugh, his eyes twinkling. "Now, no more questions. Just be ready at seven."

Emily shook her head, a mix of exasperation and amusement. "You're impossible, you know that?"

"And you love it," he shot back with a wink before turning and walking away, leaving Emily shaking her head, her curiosity only growing.

Emily rolled her eyes but couldn't help the smile that crept across her face. As the jet glided toward home, she felt a thrill of anticipation bubbling within her, wondering what Lucas had in store.

Chapter 13

As the car pulled up at the end of Emily's street, she took a deep breath, letting the familiar sight of her neighborhood calm the whirlwind inside her. She'd just returned from an emergency mission in Prague, but for her parents, she'd only been gone for a simple group project with Sophie.

Emily slipped quietly through the front door, dropping her bag by the stairs just as her mom called out, "Emily, is that you?"

"Yeah, Mom, it's me!" Emily replied, making her way into the kitchen, where the smell of roasted chicken and herbs filled the air. Her dad was setting the table, and her mom turned from the stove, a warm smile spreading across her face.

"Well, perfect timing! Just in time for supper."

Emily's heart warmed at the sight, and she realized just how much she'd missed this normalcy. "Great, I'm starving."

Her dad raised an eyebrow, chuckling. "I thought you and Sophie were working on a 'big project' all night. Did you two actually eat anything?"
Emily shrugged, stifling a smile as she slipped into her chair at the table. "Uh, you know how it is—'work hard, snack harder,'" she joked, hoping her parents couldn't sense the underlying fatigue she was trying to hide.

Her mom placed the serving dishes on the table, studying Emily's face as she did. "Well, we're just glad to have you home. You've been busier than usual, haven't you?"

Emily froze for a split second, then relaxed, letting out a soft laugh. "I guess so. But I'll be around all weekend." She caught herself almost saying, 'unless duty calls,' but quickly corrected course. "I think I'll enjoy some downtime."
Her dad passed the salad, chuckling. "Downtime and maybe some actual homework? I'm sure those teachers have noticed you've been a bit… distracted lately."
"Or maybe just saving all her energy for the weekend," her mom added with a wink, serving a spoonful of mashed potatoes onto Emily's plate.

Emily grinned, shaking her head. "You both know me too well. I'll be good—promise." She filled her plate, eager to soak in the warmth of home, her parents' easy banter, and the delicious food she hadn't had in what felt like ages.

After dinner, Emily helped with the dishes, relishing the simple routine of rinsing plates and stacking them beside her mom at the sink. The conversation was light—plans for the weekend, updates on extended family, and jokes about her dad's love for over-salting his food.

Finally, when the kitchen was spotless and the last dish was put away, Emily gave each of her parents a quick hug and excused herself to her room. She felt a rush of relief as she slipped into her room, kicking off her shoes and letting out a sigh as she sat down on her bed.

A thought nudged at her, and she picked up her phone to text Sophie.

Emily: Made it through dinner without them suspecting anything! Thanks again for covering for me. Are we still on for school tomorrow?

A few seconds later, Sophie's reply popped up.

Sophie: Of course! You better have some crazy stories to share... minus the spy details.

Emily: You know it! See you in homeroom. Night, Soph!
Sophie: Night, Em. And hey—stay out of trouble for once!

Emily laughed softly, setting her phone down on the nightstand. Her mind drifted briefly to Lucas, wondering what he could possibly have planned for the weekend. The thought made her smile, and she leaned back on her pillow, allowing herself to relax as her home felt like a safe haven once more. But deep down, she knew she was never entirely off-duty.

___ *Wednesday*

The sound of the bell echoing through the halls was a welcome relief. Emily grabbed her books from her locker and shut it with a soft thud, ready to get through the day. Her mind, however, was miles away, caught in thoughts of Lucas. The text conversation they had kept running in the background of her mind. She couldn't stop thinking about the mission, the kiss, and the way he'd said he had a surprise for her this weekend. Every time her phone buzzed, her heart skipped a beat. But she couldn't let herself get too distracted—not with a major history exam and a group project to worry about.

At lunch, Sophie slid into the seat across from her, eyebrows raised. "Okay, spill. How's your 'group project' going? I swear you've been acting like you're on a secret mission these days."

Emily laughed, shaking her head. "You're not going to believe it if I told you. But it's all under control, promise."

Sophie rolled her eyes. "You've been so cryptic lately, I'm starting to think you're moonlighting as a spy or something. I'm just trying to get through this week, and it's been insane. I need a break, and you... well, you need to stop being so secretive."

Emily forced a smile. "It's nothing, really. Just been a lot on my plate with everything, you know?"

She pulled out her phone when it buzzed, trying to keep the conversation casual. It was a text from Lucas, but she quickly hid it before Sophie could see. Sophie's eyes, though, were trained on her every move. "You're doing it again! What's up with you? Who's texting you all the time?"

Emily ignored her friend's probing questions, quickly texting Lucas back. "Hey, what's your surprise for the weekend?"

Sophie narrowed her eyes, then sighed dramatically. "Fine, keep your secrets. But if you don't tell me soon, I'll come to my own conclusions. Spy stuff, Lucas... I'm calling it."

She winked, taking a bite of her sandwich.

Emily couldn't help but laugh, feeling the pressure of keeping her secret. She knew it was only a matter of time before Sophie figured things out.

_____*Thursday*

The next day at school, Emily barely made it through her first class. She'd gotten little sleep the night before, too busy texting Lucas about the surprise he was planning for her. They hadn't said much more about it, and now the mystery was driving her crazy.

The bell rang for third period, and Emily dragged herself to history, her head buzzing.

Mr. Thompson called on her in the middle of her daze, jolting her out of her thoughts. "Ms. Carter, can you tell the class about the Treaty of Versailles and its impact on Europe?"

Emily blinked, panicking for a second, then blurted out the first thing that came to mind. "Uh, sure... The treaty essentially laid the groundwork for... tensions between nations, particularly Germany, which led to World War II. It also left France and Britain with economic problems..."

Her voice trailed off, and she glanced at her classmates, who were all staring at her. Mr. Thompson raised an eyebrow, clearly unimpressed. "Ms. Carter, please make sure you review the material before tomorrow's test."
Her face turned red as she nodded. "Right. Thanks, Mr. Thompson."

The rest of the class continued in awkward silence as Emily sank further into her seat. Sophie's eyes shot daggers at her across the room.

"I can't believe you said that! I knew you were distracted but come on..." she whispered under her breath, barely able to hide her grin.

___*Friday*

By Friday, the weight of the week finally started to settle in. Emily had barely made it through the history test and had practically passed out during her lunch period from exhaustion.

But things started to feel different by the end of the school day. The weekend was almost here, and with it, Lucas's mystery surprise. Her mind was swirling. How would she juggle this with Sophie? Would Lucas tell her more? She couldn't stop thinking about him.

As the final bell rang, Sophie walked up to Emily, a mischievous grin on her face. "Okay, I know you've been acting weird all week, and I know you're keeping something from me. But I can't take it anymore." She crossed her arms, staring Emily down. "Tell me about Lucas. Now."

Emily stopped in her tracks, her heart skipping a beat.

She'd been trying so hard to keep everything under wraps, but now, with Sophie's eyes on her, Emily realized there was no hiding it any longer. She exhaled slowly. "Fine. You've earned it." She took a deep breath and began.

"Sophie, Lucas is... He's an agent. He works for the same agency I do. We met during a mission in Paris, and—" She hesitated, feeling the weight of the truth. "And, well... things happened. I don't want to complicate things more, but it's real."

Sophie stood there, blinking in shock. "Wait... What? You're telling me that Lucas... the one you've been texting and acting all secretive about... is a spy? And he's involved with you? Like... in that way?"

Emily nodded, feeling her cheeks flush. "Yeah, it's... complicated. But it's true. He's part of my world. And I can't just ignore the feelings I have for him, even though I should be focusing on missions, not relationships."

Sophie stared at her for a long time, her mouth slightly open. Then, finally, she burst out laughing. "I can't believe this. You... you're living a freaking double life, and you've been hiding it from me for who knows how long? You're crazy, Em. But... I get it. I think. You're not some ordinary girl, are you?"

Emily sighed in relief. "I never wanted to lie to you. I promise, I didn't want to keep this from you. But it's dangerous, and I had to be careful."

Sophie leaned in and gave her a hug. "You're my best friend, and I'm here for you. Just... don't get yourself into too much trouble, okay? You've already got enough going on."

"Deal," Emily said, laughing through the tension. "But... don't be mad if I have to sneak off for a mission every now and then."

Sophie just rolled her eyes, clearly still processing. "Whatever. Just keep me in the loop next time, okay?"

That evening, Emily settled into her room, exhausted but with a weight lifted off her shoulders after telling Sophie everything. Her phone buzzed again, and this time, it was a message from Lucas. **"You still up? I'm really looking forward to this weekend."**

Emily smiled as she typed back. **"I'm in. What's the surprise?"**

The text came in almost immediately. **"Not telling yet. You'll find out soon enough. Can't wait to see you."**

Her heart raced again. What could it be? She couldn't wait for the weekend to unfold, but one thing was clear—Lucas had a plan, and Emily was all in.

Chapter 14

Saturday morning began like any other. Emily had barely finished her breakfast and was still in her pajamas when the doorbell rang. She exchanged a puzzled glance with her mom, who was clearing the table, then made her way to the door.

As she opened it, her heart nearly stopped.

There, casually leaning against the frame with a slight grin, stood Lucas.

"Hey, Emily," he greeted, his voice soft yet teasing. "Hope it's not too early?"

"Lucas!" she whispered, her eyes wide. She quickly pulled him inside, glancing over her shoulder to make sure her parents hadn't noticed her reaction. She dropped her voice even lower. "What are you doing here?"

Lucas chuckled. "You're not the only one who can pull off surprises. Thought I'd pay a visit—thought it was time I met your family."

Emily's mind raced. She hadn't been expecting this, and her heart was pounding as she looked him over. Dressed in a clean, casual sweater and jeans, Lucas looked every bit the charming guest. He even carried a gift bag with him. "Okay, but… what's the cover story?"
"Relax," Lucas reassured her with a confident smile. "We're old friends. We met at an academic camp, and I'm here in town looking at the university for next year."
Emily took a steadying breath. "Okay. I can work with that."

"Emily?" Her mom's voice carried from the kitchen. "Who's at the door?"
Emily gave Lucas a quick nod and then turned back toward the kitchen. "Mom, Dad—this is Lucas," she announced as they walked in together. "We met at that academic camp last summer."

Her mom's face brightened, her dad's curious gaze settling on Lucas with interest. "Well, any friend of Emily's is a friend of ours," her mom said warmly. "Please, come in. Would you like some breakfast? We have more than enough."

"That would be great, thank you, Mrs. Carter," Lucas replied, handing over the gift bag. "I didn't want to come empty-handed. It's just some local coffee beans and chocolate. Thought it might be a nice gesture."

Emily's mom looked delighted. "How thoughtful! Thank you, Lucas. Please, sit down and make yourself comfortable. Emily, why don't you go get changed?" She winked at her daughter. "We wouldn't want Lucas to think you don't get dressed on Saturdays."

Emily blushed, darting upstairs to change into something casual but nicer than pajamas. As she brushed her hair, she quickly texted Sophie:
Emily: You'll never believe who just showed up at my house.

Sophie's reply came almost instantly.
Sophie: OMG, who?
Emily: Lucas! He's meeting my family as my "camp friend."
Sophie: WHAT?! I need to see this! I have to pick up that book from you, anyway. Be there soon!

Emily's eyes widened. Before she could reply, she heard her mom calling from downstairs. "Emily, are you ready? Lucas was just telling us all about his plans for university." She rushed down the stairs to find Lucas seated at the table, effortlessly charming her parents.

He was discussing his "plans" for studying engineering, which conveniently matched his background with the agency.

"And you're thinking of moving here?" her dad asked, intrigued.
Lucas nodded. "That's right, Mr. Carter. I've been looking at a few places near campus. I want a place that feels like home, you know?"

As they continued chatting, the doorbell rang again. Emily's stomach did a nervous flip as she hurried to answer it, opening the door to find Sophie standing there, looking breathless and excited.

"Hey!" Sophie whispered. "Is he still here?"
"Yes, but be cool," Emily murmured back, grabbing a book from the nearby shelf and handing it to her. "Here's the book you needed. Now go before my parents—"
Just then, Lucas walked into the entryway, his warm smile extending to Sophie. "Hello, I'm Lucas," he said, holding out a hand. "You must be Sophie?"

Sophie's eyes widened in excitement as she shook his hand, her face turning a bit red. "Oh—uh, yes! Nice to meet you, Lucas."

She shot Emily a look of exaggerated intrigue.

Emily cleared her throat, nudging Sophie gently toward the door. "Well, thanks for stopping by, Soph. I'll text you later."

"Sure," Sophie replied, a sly smile on her lips as she backed out the door, giving Emily a quick wink. "Nice meeting you, Lucas. See you soon, Em."

As soon as Sophie left, Emily turned back to Lucas, who looked thoroughly amused. "Your friend seems... interesting."

Emily laughed. "Yeah, that's Sophie. She's my best friend —and very curious about everything."

Lucas chuckled, then motioned back to the kitchen. "Ready to rejoin your parents?"

After rejoining her parents, Emily and Lucas continued chatting about "camp memories" over breakfast, her parents clearly charmed by his polite and warm demeanor. They even invited him to stay a bit longer, so she offered to give him a tour of the house and yard.

"So... meeting the parents, huh?" Emily whispered as they stepped out onto the back porch.

Lucas shrugged, looking amused. "You've met mine... it's only fair, right?"

They walked through the yard, pausing by the garden. Emily glanced around, ensuring they were alone. "You really went all out with this cover story."

"Well, it's not really a cover story," he replied, his voice softening as he looked at her. "It's true. I will be moving her and going to school next year."

Emily's heart fluttered at his words. She squeezed his hand, feeling an undeniable connection in that moment, but before either of them could say more, her mom called from the back door, "Emily, we're heading out to do some shopping. Lucas, would you like to stay for supper?"
Lucas grinned and nodded. "I'd love to, Mrs. Carter."

After her parents left, he turned to Emily, a mischievous glint in his eyes. "Maybe we could catch a movie later."

After her parents left for their shopping trip, Lucas glanced around Emily's room with a small, appreciative smile. "This is where the magic happens, huh?" he teased, glancing at her neatly stacked books, her cluttered desk, and the little mementos that made the space feel cozy.

Emily laughed, shaking her head. "It's just a normal room. I doubt you'd call it magical."

Lucas moved closer, his gaze softening. "Well, it feels like you. That's what makes it special."
Emily's cheeks flushed, and she felt a warmth in her chest as he stepped even closer.

Her heart thudded as she tilted her face up to meet his gaze. Their hands found each other, and for a moment, the world faded away, leaving only the quiet intensity between them. Lucas leaned in, and their lips met in a soft, lingering kiss.

The kiss deepened, filling Emily with a mix of excitement and contentment. Lucas was gentle, thoughtful, and she felt her heart race as his hand rested lightly on her waist. He pulled back slowly, his forehead resting against hers, his voice low. "I've wanted to do that since the day we met."

Her breath caught, and she laughed softly, feeling both nervous and thrilled. "Well, I wouldn't have minded if you'd told me sooner."
Lucas chuckled, brushing a stray hair from her face. "I guess I was waiting for the right moment."

They shared a quiet smile before Lucas glanced at her posters and shelves with curiosity. "So," he said, glancing around, "show me more of your world?"

They spent the afternoon wandering through Emily's neighborhood. First, she took him to her high school, pointing out the classrooms and fields, sharing stories of classes, friends, and her teachers' quirks.

Lucas listened intently, occasionally teasing her about the overly enthusiastic way she described her achievements and minor mishaps. He seemed particularly interested in hearing about her best friend, Sophie, grinning every time Emily mentioned her name.

Next, they strolled to the local park, where Emily showed him the benches where she'd often sit with Sophie, sharing secrets or studying between laughs. The swings squeaked softly in the breeze, and they sat side by side, looking out over the small lake that sparkled in the afternoon sun.

"It's peaceful here," Lucas said, his eyes drifting over the landscape.

"Yeah," Emily replied softly. "Sometimes I come here just to think. It's a nice escape."

He glanced at her, his hand finding hers again. "I can see why you love it."

Finally, they stopped by her favorite coffee shop. The barista greeted her with a cheerful wave, and Lucas grinned as she explained her usual order. They sat by the window, sipping their drinks, exchanging lighthearted stories and quiet glances.

By the time they returned home, it was close to dinner, and Emily's parents had set the table with homemade lasagna, garlic bread, and a fresh salad. Her mom beamed as Lucas complimented the meal, and her dad asked him about his plans for university. Lucas played his role perfectly, describing his "engineering" path with just enough detail to sound convincing. Emily couldn't help but smile, amazed at how easily he fit into her life.

After dinner, as the plates were being cleared, Lucas gave her a conspiratorial grin. "So… ready for our movie date?" Emily laughed, nodding. "Absolutely. Let me grab my jacket."

They made their way to the theater, and as the lights dimmed, the irony of their movie choice dawned on them. "A spy adventure," Lucas murmured, clearly amused. "You couldn't have picked something like a rom-com?"

Emily shrugged, her eyes glinting. "Consider it research." As the movie unfolded, they exchanged knowing glances every time the characters did something wildly unrealistic or dangerously close to real-life spy protocol. Lucas whispered a few times, adding witty commentary that had Emily struggling to keep from laughing out loud. When the hero narrowly escaped capture by a hair's breadth, she nudged him with a smirk. "Does this look familiar?"

They both laughed, drawing a few annoyed glances from the other viewers, but they didn't care. The shared jokes and the thrill of the movie made it feel like they were in their own little world.

After the movie, they walked back to Emily's house under a sky dusted with stars. The air was crisp, and Lucas slipped his hand into hers, their fingers intertwining naturally. When they reached her front porch, they stopped, neither wanting the evening to end.

Lucas brushed a lock of hair from her face, his gaze soft and unwavering. "Thank you for today, Emily. It's been… unforgettable."
She smiled, her heart full. "Same here. I'm glad you came. It meant a lot to me."
Without another word, he leaned in, and their lips met in a slow, tender kiss, one that left her breathless and feeling as if she were floating. They lingered there, wrapped in the warmth of the moment, before finally pulling back, their eyes meeting with an unspoken promise.
"Goodnight, Lucas," she whispered.
"Goodnight, Emily," he replied, his voice gentle as he stepped back, giving her one last smile before heading down the steps and disappearing into the night.
As she watched him go, Emily knew that her world was never going to feel quite the same again.

Chapter 15

The week dragged by in a blur of classrooms, homework, and whispered conversations between Emily and Sophie. But Emily's mind was somewhere else entirely—on Lucas. Her phone buzzed constantly with their text exchanges, each one a small escape from the monotony of high school life.

___Monday

Lucas: Morning, superstar. What's the plan today? Algebra? Saving the world?
Emily: Mostly trying not to fall asleep in class. You?
Lucas: Studying for a final exam. Thinking about last weekend instead.
Emily: Same. I'm already counting down to Friday.
Lucas: Me too.

___*Wednesday*

Emily sat in the cafeteria, pushing her food around on her tray as she texted under the table.

Lucas: What's got you distracted today?
Emily: This history project. Also, wishing something exciting would happen. I'm about to die of boredom.
Lucas: Careful what you wish for. Excitement tends to come with alarms.
Emily: Bring it on. Anything's better than this.

By Thursday night, Emily was ready to crawl into bed and leave the uneventful week behind her. She changed into her pajamas and settled under the covers, her thoughts drifting to Lucas as she stared at her phone, hoping for one more text before falling asleep.

But instead of Lucas's name lighting up her screen, it was the agency's alert.

Agent Carter: Briefing scheduled at dawn. Mission details classified.

Emily sat upright, her heart pounding with equal parts adrenaline and anticipation. She jumped out of bed, rushing down the hall to her parents' room. Knocking lightly on the door, she poked her head inside.

"Mom? Dad?" she said, feigning urgency. "I completely forgot to tell you—we're leaving for the basketball tournament tomorrow morning. I'm so sorry I didn't mention it earlier."

Her mom blinked, half-asleep. "Tournament? Where is it again?"

"Upstate," Emily improvised, her voice steady. "We won't be back until Sunday night."

Her dad yawned, waving her off. "Just make sure you have everything packed. You'll need your uniform."

"Of course," Emily said, fighting the urge to smile. "Thanks. Goodnight!"

She darted back to her room, already mentally preparing for the mission.

The dawn light streamed into the agency's private meeting room as Emily entered, her heart racing. The screen flickered to life, revealing Benson's stern face and the mission details.

"Good morning, Agent Carter," he began. "Your mission is to intercept a group of highly organized art thieves targeting an ancient artifact. The target is housed in a museum in Rio de Janeiro, but intelligence suggests the thieves plan to smuggle it through the jungle to a private buyer."

Emily nodded, her focus sharpening. "What's my role?"
"You will track and intercept the artifact, ensuring it is returned safely. This will require jungle navigation and discreet extraction methods. You'll be working solo on the ground, but all communications will go through Agent Dupont," Benson added, his tone neutral.

Her pulse quickened at the mention of Lucas, but she kept her expression professional. "Understood, sir."

The screen shifted, and a map of Rio appeared. Benson outlined key points, including the thieves' last-known location and the likely route through the jungle.
"Good luck, Agent Carter," Benson concluded. "We'll see you on the other side."

Emily stepped off the plane into the humid air of Rio de Janeiro, her senses heightened as she blended into the bustling streets. Carnival was in full swing, the vibrant colors and music providing the perfect cover for her mission.

"Emily," Lucas's voice came through her earpiece, calm and steady. "I'm tracking your movements. The thieves are about half a mile ahead. Stay on their trail, but don't engage yet."
"Got it," she replied, weaving through the crowd.

Emily found herself deep in the dense jungle, her body aching from the relentless pursuit. The air was thick with humidity, the kind that clung to her skin and made every movement feel heavier. Towering trees created a canopy so dense that the early morning light barely filtered through, leaving her surroundings cloaked in shadow. Vines twisted down like silent sentinels, and the distant calls of unseen creatures echoed around her.

She crouched low behind a massive tree, its gnarled roots snaking across the ground like ancient veins. Ahead, the thieves had set up camp in a small clearing. A dim fire flickered at the center, casting dancing shadows over the stacks of crates and the silhouettes of three men. Two were speaking in hushed tones, while the third paced with a flashlight, the beam cutting through the underbrush.

"Lucas," she whispered into her earpiece, exhaustion creeping into her voice. "They've stopped for the night. I'll move in at first light."

"Understood," Lucas replied, his voice steady but softer now. "You're doing great. Get some rest while you can."

Her heart warmed at his words, a brief moment of comfort in the otherwise hostile jungle.
"Thanks, Lucas. Talk to you in the morning."

She settled into the shadows, careful to keep her movements quiet. But just as she shifted, a sudden crack of a branch nearby made her freeze. Her eyes darted to the clearing. The pacing thief stopped, his flashlight snapping toward the noise. The beam swept dangerously close to her hiding spot.

Emily's breath hitched as the man stepped toward her, muttering something to his companions. She pressed herself against the tree's rough bark, her fingers instinctively brushing the hilt of her knife. The rustling in the bushes grew louder, and she tensed, ready to act if necessary.

Then, with an audible hiss, a massive jungle snake slithered out from the foliage. Its dark, scaled body shimmered in the firelight as it coiled slowly, its forked tongue flicking out to taste the air.

"Snake!" one of the thieves shouted, stumbling back. His panic sent the camp into chaos. The other two drew their weapons, their fear palpable as they barked orders at one another, but none of them dared approach the snake.

Emily stayed perfectly still, watching as the reptile moved lazily toward the fire, unbothered by the noise. The distraction gave her the perfect opportunity.

She slid further into the shadows, her movements slow and deliberate, until she was far enough away to avoid detection.

Several minutes later, she found a spot to rest—a hollow beneath the roots of an ancient tree. Thick vines and ferns partially enclosed the space, creating a natural shelter that offered both cover and a clear view of the thieves' camp in the distance. The ground was damp but soft, covered in moss that smelled faintly of earth and decay.

Emily crouched low, scanning her surroundings. The jungle was alive with sound now, a symphony of croaks, chirps, and distant howls that seemed to grow louder as the sun dipped below the horizon.
Fireflies blinked like tiny lanterns, their light dancing against the darkness.

She lay down carefully, her head resting against one of the tree's thick roots. The knife stayed within arm's reach, and her earpiece remained in place. She knew sleep wouldn't come easily—not here, not with the jungle teeming with life and the thieves so close.

But she had to try. She let her eyes close, the rhythmic sounds of the jungle lulling her into a light, uneasy slumber. Her thoughts lingered briefly on Lucas, his steady voice a comforting presence even from miles away.

With one eye metaphorically open, she let the night envelop her, knowing the real challenge would come with the first light of dawn.

———

The first faint glow of dawn seeped through the jungle canopy, painting the dense foliage with soft hues of gold and green. Emily's eyes fluttered open, her senses immediately on high alert. She stretched her cramped limbs carefully, the damp moss beneath her pressing against her skin. The thieves' camp was still visible in the clearing ahead, the fire now reduced to glowing embers. The three men were sprawled around it, fast asleep.

This was her moment.

Emily moved silently, her every step deliberate. Her boots barely made a sound on the soft jungle floor as she edged closer to the camp. The crates holding the stolen artifact sat just a few feet from the nearest thief. She crouched low, her breath shallow, and slipped behind one of the larger crates, scanning the area for traps or alarms.

Her fingers found the latch on the crate marked with the artifact's symbol—a coiled serpent. Slowly, she eased it open, revealing the prize inside: an ancient jade idol, its intricate carvings glinting faintly in the low light.

It was smaller than she'd expected, fitting neatly into the bag she carried.

The sound of one of the thieves shifting in his sleep made her freeze, her pulse quickening. She waited, barely daring to breathe, as the man muttered something incoherent before settling again. Relieved, Emily closed the crate carefully and melted back into the shadows, the artifact secure in her pack.

"Lucas," she whispered into her earpiece as she moved quickly but quietly away from the camp. "I've got the artifact. Heading out now."

"Great work," Lucas's voice crackled softly in her ear. "You need to head east. I've located a narrow road about a kilometer from your position. It's not on the maps, but it should get you back to civilization."

"Got it," Emily replied, her voice steady despite the adrenaline coursing through her veins.

The jungle seemed alive around her, every sound amplified in the early morning quiet. Birds called overhead, and the distant hum of insects provided a constant backdrop. Emily pushed through thick underbrush, ducking beneath low-hanging vines and stepping carefully over gnarled roots. Her muscles ached, but she kept moving, the thought of the thieves waking spurring her forward.

"Emily," Lucas's voice came again, calm but firm. "You've got company. Looks like one of the thieves woke up. He's on your trail."

Emily's heart leapt, but she forced herself to remain calm. "How far?"

"About two hundred meters behind you. Keep moving; I'll guide you."

She quickened her pace, her eyes scanning for landmarks or signs of the road Lucas had mentioned. The sound of rustling behind her grew louder, and she cursed under her breath. She needed to lose him.

Chapter 16

Spotting a dense thicket to her right, Emily veered off the path and crouched low, her body hidden by the thick foliage. She waited, her breath coming in controlled, silent intervals. Moments later, the thief stumbled past, his attention focused ahead. Emily allowed herself a small, relieved smile before slipping back onto her original path.

The road came into view just as Lucas's voice returned. "You're almost there. Good timing—a bus is heading your way. Wave it down."

Emily emerged from the jungle, her boots hitting the dusty road just as an old, battered bus rumbled into sight. Its sides were painted with faded colors, and the roof was piled high with sacks, crates, and even a few clucking chickens.

She raised her hand, and the driver brought the vehicle to a screeching halt. The door creaked open, and a middle-aged man with a wide-brimmed hat peered down at her.

"Rio?" Emily asked in Portuguese, her accent passable.
The man nodded, gesturing for her to climb aboard. She did, slipping into an empty seat near the back. The bus was packed with villagers, farmers, and their goods. A small boy sitting across from her stared curiously, while a chicken perched precariously on a crate beside him flapped its wings.

Emily leaned back, grateful for the brief respite. The jade idol was secured in her pack, and she allowed herself a small smile of accomplishment. But the peace didn't last long.

The bus jolted to a stop, throwing Emily forward in her seat. Shouts echoed from outside, followed by the clatter of boots on the road. She peered through the dirty window and felt her stomach drop. A group of armed men, their faces partially obscured by scarves, approached the bus. Jungle rebels.
"Lucas," she whispered, her voice urgent. "We've got a problem."
"Stay calm," he replied immediately. "Don't draw attention to yourself."

The rebels began boarding the bus, their rifles slung casually over their shoulders. They barked orders in rapid Portuguese, demanding identification from the passengers. Emily lowered her head, pulling the brim of her borrowed cap down to shield her face.

One of the rebels stopped near her seat, his eyes narrowing as he scanned the passengers. Emily's heart pounded as his gaze lingered on her for a moment too long. Her hand tightened around the small knife hidden in her jacket, but she forced herself to remain still.

A loud squawk broke the tension as the chicken beside the boy flapped wildly, knocking over a crate. The rebel turned, distracted by the commotion, and barked at the boy to settle the bird. Taking advantage of the moment, Emily slid further down in her seat, her face turned toward the window.

After a tense few minutes, the rebels exited the bus, waving it on. The driver didn't hesitate, slamming the accelerator and speeding down the road. Emily exhaled slowly, her muscles finally relaxing.

As the bus rumbled into the outskirts of Rio, Emily spotted the safe house Lucas had marked on her map. She tapped the driver on the shoulder and thanked him before disembarking. The city noise was a welcome change from the oppressive quiet of the jungle.

"Lucas, I'm clear," she said into her earpiece, relief washing over her.

"Good work, Emily," he replied. "Head to the safe house, and we'll arrange extraction from there."

She adjusted her pack, her steps steady as she made her way toward the next phase of her mission. The adrenaline had subsided, but her focus remained sharp. The artifact was safe, and so was she—for now.

The outskirts of Rio buzzed with activity as Emily weaved her way through the narrow, bustling streets. The safe house was tucked away in a quieter part of the city, far from the noise and chaos. The map Lucas had provided guided her step by step, though she kept her senses sharp, scanning her surroundings for any sign of trouble.

As she walked, the enticing smell of grilled meat and spices drifted through the air, her empty stomach growling in response. She stopped at a small food cart, where a cheerful vendor flipped sizzling skewers of meat over a makeshift grill.

"Bom dia," the man greeted, flashing a wide smile. "You look hungry."

"Famished," Emily replied, forcing a smile. She handed over a few reais and took the skewer, savoring the smoky aroma as she bit into the tender meat.

But something felt off.

The vendor's friendly demeanor lingered a moment too long, his eyes flicking to the small pack on her back. Emily pretended not to notice, finishing her skewer quickly before slipping back into the crowd. As she turned a corner, her suspicions were confirmed—someone was following her.

"Lucas," she murmured into her earpiece, her voice tight. "I've got a tail."

"How close?" he asked, his tone instantly serious.

"About twenty feet back. Male. Mid-thirties. Probably armed."

"Don't lead him to the safe house," Lucas instructed. "Lose him first."

Easier said than done, Emily thought as she ducked into a side alley. The narrow passage was lined with crumbling walls and faded graffiti. She quickened her pace, her heart pounding as her footsteps echoed against the cobblestones. The tail followed, his boots crunching louder with each step. Emily turned another corner, leading him through a maze of alleys before doubling back and slipping through a hidden side entrance to the safe house.

Emily bolted the door behind her, setting her pack on the table. She couldn't shake the feeling that she wasn't alone. Her pulse quickened as she heard a faint creak from the back window.

The intruder had found her.

The man from the food cart stepped into the room, his face twisted in a smug grin. "You've got something that doesn't belong to you," he said in accented English, his hand resting on the hilt of a knife tucked into his belt.

Emily's eyes narrowed as she shifted her stance, her body tensing for a fight. "And I'm guessing you're here to take it?"

"That's the idea," he replied, stepping closer.

The man lunged, but Emily was ready. She sidestepped quickly, grabbing a chair and slamming it into his midsection. He staggered back, cursing in Portuguese. The artifact was still in her pack on the table, and she couldn't let him get near it.

He came at her again, swinging wildly. Emily ducked, her training kicking in as she drove her elbow into his ribs. He grunted in pain but managed to grab her arm, twisting it painfully. She spun, using his momentum to throw him off balance, and delivered a swift kick to his knee. He crumpled, but his hand shot out, grabbing the strap of her pack.

"Lucas, I need extraction—now!" she shouted into her earpiece, grappling for control of the bag.

"Hang tight," Lucas's voice came through, steady and calm despite the chaos. "Team's en route."

The thief yanked the bag free, but Emily didn't hesitate. She launched herself at him, slamming him into the wall. The pack fell to the ground, and Emily grabbed it, retreating quickly as the man scrambled to his feet. Before he could charge again, the sound of pounding boots echoed from outside.

The extraction team burst through the door, their weapons trained on the intruder. He froze, his hands slowly raising in surrender. Emily exhaled sharply, clutching the pack tightly as the agents secured the thief and ushered him out.

———

Emily slumped into a plush seat on the private jet, the adrenaline slowly draining from her system. The artifact was secured in a case beside her, its significance weighing heavily on her mind. She activated her tablet, connecting to the debriefing video call.

Benson's face appeared on the screen, his expression stern. "Agent Carter, I understand there was some... additional excitement at the safe house?"

"Yes, sir," Emily replied, her voice steady despite her exhaustion. She recounted the events in detail, her professionalism masking the lingering tension.

"Well done," Benson said after a pause. "The artifact is safe, and the thief is in custody. Mission accomplished."

As the call ended, only Lucas remained on the line. His face softened, and the corners of his mouth lifted in a faint smile. "You really know how to keep things interesting, don't you?"

Emily laughed softly, leaning back in her seat. "You have no idea. Thanks for the navigation, by the way. Couldn't have done it without you."

"Anytime," Lucas replied, his voice low and warm. "You okay?"

"Tired," she admitted. "But I'll survive. You?"

"Same," he said, leaning closer to the camera. "Wish I could've been there, though."

Emily felt her cheeks flush, a warmth spreading through her despite the cool air of the plane. "You were there. In a way."

They talked quietly for the remainder of the flight, their conversation slipping into personal territory—dreams, favorite movies, and memories from past missions. Emily felt the tension of the mission melt away, replaced by the comfort of Lucas's voice.

——

Emily stepped through her front door just as her parents were settling into the living room. She dropped her duffel bag by the stairs, offering them a tired smile.

"How was the tournament?" her mom asked, looking up from the couch.

"Exhausting," Emily replied honestly, flopping onto the nearest chair. "We didn't win, but it was a good experience." Her dad chuckled. "Well, we're proud of you. Now, get some rest—you look like you've been through the wringer."

Emily smiled, nodding as she made her way upstairs. Once in her room, she collapsed onto her bed, her phone buzzing softly with a text.

Lucas: Get some sleep, superstar. You earned it.

She smiled, typing back quickly.

Emily: Thanks, Lucas. Talk tomorrow?

Lucas: Wouldn't miss it. Sweet dreams.

As she drifted off to sleep, Emily's thoughts lingered on the artifact, the mission, and Lucas. It wasn't a normal life, but it was hers—and she wouldn't trade it for anything.

Chapter 17

Emily slipped into her usual seat in history class, her notebook open but untouched. Mr. Callahan stood at the front of the room, regaling the class with anecdotes from his vacation in Brazil. Emily barely paid attention until his next words froze her in place.

"You know, I could have sworn I saw someone I recognized at Carnival," he said, a bemused smile on his face. "Looked just like our own Emily Carter."

The class erupted into laughter, with several students turning to look at her. Emily forced a grin, her heart hammering in her chest. "Me? At Carnival? I wish! Must have been someone else."

"Maybe it was your doppelgänger," one of her classmates teased.

Mr. Callahan chuckled and moved on with the lesson, but Emily couldn't shake the uneasy feeling. Had he really seen her? Was it just a coincidence? Or was her cover starting to crack?

———

Later that day, Emily met Sophie in the cafeteria. Sophie was already sitting with Mia, her new friend, laughing at something on her phone. Emily hesitated before joining them, her usual confidence faltering.

"Hey, Em!" Sophie greeted brightly. "We were just talking about this amazing brunch place Mia took me to last weekend. You'd love it."

Emily forced a smile. "Sounds great. Maybe we can all go sometime."

Mia glanced at Sophie, then back at Emily, her smile polite but reserved. "Sure," she said, her tone noncommittal.

The conversation moved on, but Emily couldn't shake the feeling of being an outsider. She picked at her food, her mind racing with guilt and jealousy. Sophie's laugh, usually a source of comfort, now felt like a reminder of how much she'd missed.

As lunch ended, Sophie caught Emily's arm. "Hey, you okay? You've been really quiet."

Emily hesitated, then nodded. "Yeah, just tired. Lots of homework."
Sophie's brow furrowed, but she didn't press further. "Well, let me know if you want to hang out. Mia and I are going to a movie this weekend. You should come."
"Maybe," Emily replied, her voice distant.

As Sophie turned back to Mia, laughing at something on her phone, Emily lingered for a moment, watching them. A wave of regret washed over her, tugging at her chest. She missed this—the ease of spending time with Sophie, the simple joys of being a normal teenager. It wasn't just jealousy over Mia, though that certainly stung. It was the realization that she'd been so consumed by her secret life that she'd begun losing the one part of her world that felt real.

Emily walked away, her thoughts spinning. What would it be like to have a weekend without missions, without constant vigilance? To just sit in a movie theater with her best friend and laugh until her sides hurt? The envy crept in, unbidden and sharp. She'd never admit it out loud, but sometimes she wished she could trade the adrenaline of espionage for the predictability of normal life.
She glanced at her phone, almost expecting the agency's alert to pop up any second. It hadn't yet, but she knew it was only a matter of time.

A mission always came, pulling her further from the life she pretended to have. And when it did, she'd have to come up with another excuse, another lie, further straining the fragile threads of her friendship with Sophie.

Emily sighed, stuffing her hands into her pockets as she made her way to her next class. Whatever the weekend held, she doubted it would involve anything as simple as a movie night.

That evening, Sophie called, her tone more serious than usual. "Emily, what's going on with you? You've been so distant lately, and it feels like you're pulling away."

Emily's stomach twisted. "I'm not pulling away. Things have just been... complicated."

"Complicated how?" Sophie pressed. "I've tried to include you, but you're always busy or distracted. Do you even want to hang out anymore?"

Emily sighed, the weight of her secret life pressing down on her. "It's not like that. I do want to hang out. I just... I've got a lot going on."

"Like what?" Sophie's voice cracked with frustration. "You're not telling me anything. You're my best friend, Emily, but it feels like you don't trust me anymore."

Emily's throat tightened. "I do trust you, Soph. I just... can't explain right now."

"Fine," Sophie said after a long pause. "But don't expect me to keep waiting around. I can't be the only one trying to hold this friendship together."

The call ended, leaving Emily staring at her phone, guilt and sadness twisting in her chest.

The next morning, Emily noticed a dark sedan parked across the street from the park on the way to school. As she passed, it started to move.

At school, Emily's tension mounted. She spotted a figure lingering near the entrance, his stance too rigid and deliberate to be casual. He seemed to be watching the students filter in, his eyes scanning the crowd as if looking for someone. Emily avoided his gaze, slipping inside quickly, her pulse racing.

Later in the day, as she made her way to her next class, she noticed the same man in the hallway. He wasn't dressed like a teacher or staff member, and the way he leaned against the wall, pretending to check his phone, set her instincts on edge. As she walked past, he glanced up, and their eyes met for a brief moment. His gaze was sharp, assessing, and it sent a chill down her spine.

By the time the final bell rang, her nerves were frayed. She hurried out of the building, hoping to lose herself in the throng of students, but suddenly she was shoved from behind. When she turned, she saw the man walking away.

She notice her bag was open.

Once she was safely away, Emily ducked into an empty corner of the library to check her bag. Inside was a single black card, its surface smooth and cold. The word "**WATCHING**" was printed in stark white letters, bold and unmissable.

Emily's breath caught, her chest tightening as she stared at the card. A chill ran down her spine. She felt exposed, vulnerable, as though someone had been tracking her every move all day.

She grabbed her phone and found a quiet study room, locking the door behind her. Her fingers hovered over the keypad before she dialed the agency's emergency line. The familiar voice of Benson answered almost immediately.

"Agent Carter," Benson said, his tone neutral. "What's the situation?"

Emily's words tumbled out, rapid and breathless. "There's a man who's been following me all day—at the school entrance, in the hallways, and outside after classes. He slipped something into my bag. It's a card. It says 'WATCHING.'"

Benson was silent for a moment before replying, his voice calm but firm. "Describe the card."

"It's black, smooth, with white letters," Emily said, gripping the phone tighter.

"Anything else? Did he say anything or try to engage you?" Benson asked.

"No. He just watched me. It's like he wanted me to find the card."
Benson exhaled audibly. "We'll analyze the situation. This could be a scare tactic, or it could be an early warning. Either way, you're under surveillance."

"What do I do?" Emily asked, her voice tight with anxiety.
"Stay vigilant," Benson instructed. "Avoid unnecessary risks, keep your movements routine, and report anything unusual immediately. We'll dispatch a team to monitor the area discreetly. Until then, don't engage. Understood?"
Emily swallowed hard. "Understood."
"Good," Benson said. "You're not alone in this, Carter. Trust the process."

The line disconnected, leaving Emily in the silence of the study room. She placed the card on the desk, staring at it as unease crept through her. Her instincts screamed that this wasn't just a scare tactic. Someone was watching her—and they weren't going to stop.

——

The next morning, Emily noticed Mr. Callahan standing near the parking lot after school. He wasn't alone.

A man in a sharp suit with an intense demeanor stood with him, his posture stiff and deliberate. Emily ducked behind a tree, watching as they exchanged what looked like a folder before parting ways.

Emily pulled out her phone, her fingers flying over the keyboard.

Emily: Lucas, I think we've got a problem.

Her phone buzzed almost immediately. Lucas's name lit up the screen, and she answered in a low whisper. "Lucas."

"What's going on?" His voice was calm but carried an edge of urgency.

Emily peeked around the tree, her heart racing. "Mr. Callahan. He's talking to someone outside the school. The guy doesn't belong here. Sharp suit, intense vibe, definitely not a parent or teacher. They just exchanged something—a folder, I think."

Lucas was quiet for a beat, then spoke, his tone measured. "Keep your distance. Do not engage. We'll analyze this from our end. Just stay safe, Emily."

"What if it's connected to the surveillance?" she pressed, her eyes never leaving the pair as the suited man walked away.

"It might be," Lucas admitted. "But you need to let us handle it. Your cover's too important to risk. Don't do anything risky, okay?"

Emily sighed, the tension in her chest refusing to ease. "Fine. But this doesn't feel right, Lucas."
"I know," he replied softly. "We'll get to the bottom of it. Just trust me."

As Mr. Callahan walked away, Emily's resolve hardened. She couldn't ignore the growing signs that her cover was in jeopardy. With tensions mounting at school, at home, and within the agency, she knew the stakes had never been higher. It was time to find out exactly who was watching her—before it was too late.

Chapter 18

The text arrived late Friday night, just as Emily was finishing up her homework. She was sprawled across her bed, highlighting notes for Monday's history test, when her phone buzzed. The message was short and cryptic, but its meaning was clear:

Mission Briefing: Saturday, 0600 hours. Immediate action required.

Her stomach flipped. This was different. Usually, she received more notice. Whatever the mission was, it couldn't wait.

Emily took a deep breath and headed downstairs, where her parents were watching a movie in the living room. She hesitated in the doorway, mentally rehearsing her excuse.

"Hey, Mom, Dad," she began, her tone casual. "I've got something I need to tell you."

Her mom muted the TV, glancing up with a curious smile. "What's up, sweetie?"

"Remember how I mentioned that leadership camp I signed up for at school?" Emily said, trying to sound as nonchalant as possible.

Her dad raised an eyebrow. "Leadership camp? I don't think I remember that."

"Well, it's kind of last-minute," Emily continued quickly. "They had a spot open up, and I volunteered to go. It's this weekend, and we're leaving early tomorrow morning. I'll be back Sunday night."

Her mom looked skeptical but didn't press. "Are you sure you're not overloading yourself? You've been so busy lately."

"I'm fine," Emily assured her, mustering a bright smile. "It's just one weekend, and it'll look great on college applications."

Her dad sighed, but there was a hint of pride in his voice. "All right. Just make sure you're packed and ready to go. And check in with us, okay?"

"Of course," Emily said, relief flooding through her. "Thanks, guys. Goodnight!"

Back in her bedroom, Emily reached for her phone, typing out a quick message to Sophie:

Emily: Hey Soph, I can't make it to the movies this weekend. Mission just came through.

The reply came almost instantly:

Sophie: Again?! Em, I swear, do they ever give you a break?

Emily: I know, I'm sorry. I promise we'll hang out soon. Next weekend, my treat.

There was a pause before Sophie's reply came:

Sophie: Fine, but you owe me big time. Be careful, okay?

Emily stared at the screen, her chest tightening. She was grateful Sophie knew the truth, but it didn't make leaving any easier.

The agency's jet was already waiting on the private tarmac as Emily arrived at dawn. She climbed aboard, her adrenaline kicking in as she took her seat. The interior of the plane was sleek and functional, with screens lining the walls and a small conference area at the center.

Benson's face appeared on the main monitor as the jet taxied down the runway. His expression was as serious as she'd ever seen it.

"Agent Carter," he began, his voice steady. "This mission is of the highest priority. We have intelligence that a rogue agent, codenamed Shadow, is planning to detonate an EMP device in a major urban center. If they succeed, the attack would cripple critical infrastructure and plunge the area into chaos."

Emily leaned forward, her mind racing. "Do we know where he's operating from?"

Benson nodded, a map appearing on the screen. "Shadow was last traced to an abandoned industrial complex outside Prague. The location is heavily fortified, and we believe he has a team of mercenaries working with him. Your objective is to infiltrate the site, neutralize Shadow, and secure the device."

"Will I have backup?" Emily asked, her voice steady despite the weight of the mission.

"Yes," Benson replied. "Agents Dupont and Reyes will handle perimeter control and extraction. You'll be the primary operative on the ground."

Emily's stomach tightened. She'd handled dangerous missions before, but this felt different. Shadow wasn't just another target; he was one of their own. She couldn't afford to make a mistake.

"Understood," she said, her resolve hardening. "I'll get it done."

The screen blinked off, leaving Emily alone with her thoughts as the plane soared toward Prague. She glanced out the window, the sunrise painting the sky in shades of gold and crimson.

The beauty of the moment felt oddly at odds with the danger ahead.

By the time the jet landed, Emily was in full mission mode. Dressed in tactical gear and armed with the latest surveillance tech, she moved quickly through the shadows of the industrial complex. The air was cold and smelled faintly of oil and rust.

Her comms crackled in her ear as Lucas's voice came through. "Emily, perimeter's clear. Shadow's in the main control room on the second floor. Mercenaries are stationed throughout the building. Be careful."

"Got it," she whispered, slipping through a side entrance.

The interior was a maze of crumbling walls and machinery, the dim lighting casting long, eerie shadows. Emily moved silently, her senses heightened. She avoided a patrol of guards, ducking behind a stack of crates as they passed.

Reaching the control room, she spotted Shadow through a cracked window. He was tall and imposing, his movements calculated as he worked at a control panel. The EMP device sat on a table nearby, its ominous glow sending a shiver down her spine.

"I've got eyes on Shadow," she whispered into her comms. "Moving in."

"Be quick," Lucas replied. "Reinforcements are heading your way."

Emily slipped inside, her heart pounding as she approached the table. She was almost within reach of the device when Shadow turned, his eyes narrowing as he spotted her.

"Agent Carter," he said, his voice dripping with disdain. "I was wondering when they'd send someone to stop me."
Emily didn't hesitate. She lunged for the device, but Shadow was faster, blocking her with a brutal kick that sent her sprawling. She rolled to her feet, her knife flashing as she slashed at him, but he parried effortlessly.

The fight was fierce and unrelenting, their movements a blur of strikes and counterstrikes. Shadow was strong, but Emily's agility gave her an edge. She feinted left, then delivered a sharp blow to his side, making him stagger.

"You're good," Shadow admitted, his voice laced with mockery. "But not good enough."

Emily ignored his taunts, focusing on the device. She spotted a weak point in its casing and reached for her EMP disruptor, activating it just as Shadow lunged again. The device sparked and went dark, its threat neutralized.
Shadow roared in frustration, but Emily didn't give him a chance to recover. She delivered a final, decisive blow, knocking him unconscious.

"Target neutralized," she said into her comms, breathing hard. "Device secure."

Before she could step back, a sharp noise behind her made her whirl around. A figure emerged from the shadows. In seconds, she was captured and dragged deeper into the complex...

Chapter 19

Emily's relief at securing the device was short-lived. As she turned to leave, a sharp noise behind her made her freeze. She spun around to see two mercenaries advancing, their weapons raised. Before she could react, one of them slammed the butt of his rifle into her side, sending her crashing to the floor.

Pain shot through her ribs as she gasped, clutching her side. Her earpiece crackled to life, and Dupont's voice filled her ear. "Emily? What's going on? Report!"
"Ambush," she managed to whisper, her voice shaky. "Two… armed…"
"Stay calm," Dupont said, his voice steadier than she felt. "Help is coming. Do not engage further."
One of the mercenaries yanked the earpiece from her ear and crushed it underfoot.

Emily's heart sank as Dupont's voice was silenced. The mercenaries tied her hands behind her back with coarse rope, the fibers biting into her wrists.

"Get up," one of them barked. When she didn't move fast enough, he hauled her to her feet.
As they dragged her out of the room, her eyes darted to the now-disabled EMP device. At least that part of the mission was a success. But her relief was overshadowed by the dread coursing through her veins.

The mercenaries shoved Emily into a cold, damp room lit by a single flickering bulb. The metal chair they forced her into was bolted to the floor, and the smell of mildew filled the air. Her heart pounded as one of them loomed over her, his scarred face twisted into a cruel grin.

"We know who you are," he sneered. "Agent Carter, isn't it? You've caused us quite a bit of trouble."
Emily said nothing, meeting his gaze with defiance. Her silence seemed to enrage him. He slammed his fist on the table in front of her, making her flinch.
"You're going to tell us who sent you," he growled. "And how many more are coming."
When Emily didn't respond, the other mercenary stepped forward, holding a knife. He twirled it lazily in his hand, the blade catching the light.

Maybe a little encouragement will loosen your tongue."
Emily clenched her jaw, bracing herself. Pain radiated through her shoulder as he pressed the blade just hard enough to break the skin. She bit back a cry, refusing to give them the satisfaction.

"You're tougher than you look," the first man said, a hint of respect in his voice. "But everyone breaks eventually."

Time dragged on, each moment filled with pain and fear. Just as Emily's vision blurred from exhaustion, a distant commotion jolted her back to alertness. The faint sound of gunfire grew louder, and the mercenaries exchanged uneasy glances.
"Stay here," one of them ordered the other before stepping out. Seconds later, there was a sharp cry, followed by the thud of a body hitting the ground.
The door burst open, and Dupont strode in, his weapon raised. His eyes locked on Emily, and a flicker of relief crossed his face.

"Get your hands off her," he barked, firing a warning shot that ricocheted off the wall.
The remaining mercenary lunged for his weapon, but Dupont was faster. He disarmed the man with a precise shot, then delivered a swift punch that sent him sprawling. Emily slumped in her chair, her strength nearly gone.

Dupont was at her side in an instant, cutting through her bindings. "You okay?" he asked, his voice softer now.

"I've been better," Emily muttered, managing a weak smile. "The device is secure."

"Good," Dupont said, helping her to her feet. "Let's get out of here."

The extraction didn't go as smoothly as planned. As their vehicle sped through the narrow countryside roads, Dupont kept glancing in the rearview mirror, his jaw tightening. "We've got tails," he muttered.

Emily, though exhausted, forced herself to sit up straighter. "How many?"

"Two vehicles," Reyes confirmed from the front passenger seat, gripping his weapon. "They're not backing off."

The chase intensified as Reyes directed Dupont to take a winding backroad through the forested hills. The trees closed in around them, branches scraping the windows like ghostly fingers. After a nerve-wracking hour of weaving through the dense terrain, the pursuing vehicles were nowhere to be seen.

Dupont slowed the car as they approached a secluded cabin, barely visible in the moonlight. The building was small and weathered, tucked away in the woods like a forgotten relic.

"We'll hole up here for the night," he said, pulling up to the side of the cabin and cutting the engine. "We can't risk heading back to the jet until morning."

Emily followed him inside, her legs heavy with exhaustion. The interior was sparse, with a single bed, a couch, and a tiny bathroom. The faint smell of woodsmoke lingered in the air, and a chill crept through the drafty walls.

"We'll take shifts," Dupont said. "You need to rest. There's a shower in there if you want to clean up."

Emily nodded, her body aching with every step. She grabbed the duffel bag Reyes had left her, pulling out a clean shirt and pants before slipping into the bathroom. The hot water was a welcome relief, washing away the grime and blood of the mission. For a moment, she let herself relax, the sound of the water drowning out the chaos of the past few hours.

Emily was lost in her thoughts, steam curling around her as the hot water pounded against her shoulders. She didn't hear the door creak open until a familiar voice broke through the haze.

"Emily," Lucas called softly, his tone hesitant yet steady.
She froze, her pulse quickening. "Lucas? What are you doing here?"

The door clicked shut behind him, and she peeked out from behind the curtain, her cheeks flushed—not just from the steam. He stood there, his usual cocky demeanor replaced by something more vulnerable.

"Hey, I just wanted to make sure you're okay," he said, his eyes meeting hers through the thin veil of steam.

"Couldn't it wait until I was done?" she asked, though her voice lacked its usual sharpness.

Lucas smiled, the corner of his lips lifting in that way that always managed to disarm her. "Probably. But I wanted to make sure you're okay."

Emily sighed, the tension in her shoulders easing despite herself. "I'm fine, Lucas. You shouldn't have come all this way. Usually, you just send the rescue team."

He stepped closer, his gaze softening. "You don't get it, do you? I couldn't stay back after what happened."

Her heart twisted at the sincerity in his voice. The steam blurred the edges of her vision, making the moment feel like a dream. She let the shower curtain open, exposing her whole body to Lucas. "I'm okay," she said again, quieter this time.

Their eyes connected and the attraction was undeniable.

Lucas nodded, his eyes lingering on her glistening body for a moment longer before he turned. "I'll be out here when your done."

As the door closed behind him, Emily leaned against the tile wall, her heart racing for reasons that had nothing to do with the mission. She finished her shower quickly, wrapping herself in a towel and stepping into the room to find him waiting, sitting on the edge of the bed.

Lucas looked up as she entered, his expression softening. "Better?"

"Much," she said, sitting down beside him. The silence stretched, filled with unspoken words.

"I meant what I said," he finally said, his voice low. "Hearing about what you went through today… it scared me."

Emily turned to him, her gaze searching his. "You don't think I'm capable?"

"That's not it," he said quickly. "You're the most capable person I know. But you're also…" He hesitated, his hand brushing hers. "You're more than just a mission to me, Emily."

Her breath caught, her mind racing as she processed his words. "Lucas…"

"I don't expect you to feel the same way," he continued, his voice steady but laced with vulnerability. "But I needed you to know."

Emily's heart felt like it might burst. She placed her hand over his, her fingers trembling slightly.

"I do feel the same," she admitted, her voice barely above a whisper. "I just… I don't know what this means."

Lucas smiled, a rare, genuine smile that made her chest ache. "It means we figure it out. Together."

Chapter 20

The alarm blared, jarring Emily from the few hours of sleep she'd managed to steal. Her body ached in protest as she rolled out of bed, the events of the weekend flashing through her mind. She'd barely made it home before dawn, stumbling into her room as the first rays of sunlight crept through her window. Now, it was Monday, and school awaited.

Emily groaned, brushing her tangled hair out of her face. She threw on a hoodie and jeans, her go-to outfit when exhaustion hit, and grabbed her bag. She glanced at her phone—there was already a text from Lucas.
Lucas: Good luck surviving today. Bet you'll ace it as always.

Her lips curled into a small smile as she typed back.

Emily: Ace what? Staying awake in homeroom?
His reply was instant.
Lucas: Exactly. Let me know if you need me to "call you in sick."

Emily chuckled under her breath as she stuffed her phone into her pocket and headed downstairs. Her parents were at the table, sipping coffee and reading the newspaper. They greeted her with warm smiles, oblivious to the whirlwind of her double life.

"Morning, sweetheart," her mom said. "You look tired. Big weekend at the leadership camp?"

"You could say that," Emily mumbled, grabbing a piece of toast. "Just glad it's over."

Her dad folded his paper. "Last week of school—any plans for the summer?"
Emily hesitated, her stomach knotting. She had no idea what the agency had planned for her, but she couldn't tell them that. "Not yet. I'll figure it out," she said, kissing her mom on the cheek before heading out the door.

The school hallways buzzed with energy. The last week of classes meant students were more unruly than usual, their minds already on summer break. Emily slipped into her homeroom, dropping her bag on the desk and collapsing into her seat. Sophie was already there, scribbling something in her notebook.

"You look like you got hit by a truck," Sophie said, raising an eyebrow. "Rough weekend?"

"You have no idea," Emily muttered, resting her head on her arms.

Sophie leaned closer, her voice lowering. "Seriously, are you okay? Did… everything go as planned?"

Emily nodded slightly. "Yeah, just… a lot. I'll tell you later."

Sophie gave her a skeptical look but didn't press. The bell rang, signaling the start of class. Emily sat through the lecture in a daze, her mind drifting to Lucas. A memory of his voice, his touch, flickered through her thoughts, making her heart skip a beat. She glanced at her phone under the desk, tempted to text him, but resisted.

The day dragged on, each class blending into the next. By lunchtime, Emily felt like a zombie, barely keeping her eyes open as she sat with Sophie in the cafeteria. She was about to take a bite of her sandwich when her phone buzzed. It was from Benson.

Benson: Briefing. 8 PM. Confidential.

Her heart raced. *What now?*

She texted back a quick acknowledgment, shoving her phone into her pocket before Sophie noticed. She forced a smile, but her appetite was gone.

By the time she got home, Emily's nerves were frayed. She excused herself from dinner early, retreating to her room and logging into the secure agency portal on her laptop. Benson's face appeared on the screen, his expression unreadable.

"Agent Carter," he began. "Your performance over the past year has been exemplary. The agency has selected you for an elite summer training program at our academy in England."

Emily's eyes widened. "England? When does it start?"
"In two weeks," Benson replied. "This isn't just any training program. It's an opportunity to advance your skills and prepare for high-stakes missions. Only the best are invited."
Emily swallowed hard, excitement and dread warring within her. "I… I'm honored."
"You should be," Benson said, his tone softening slightly. "Pack accordingly. Dismissed."
The screen went dark, and Emily sat back, staring at her reflection in the blank screen. England. Training. It felt surreal, but there was no time to process it.

Emily lay back on her bed, staring at the ceiling as the enormity of the situation sank in. England. The academy. The whole summer. Her mind raced as she considered what it would mean for her double life.

The cover story has to be perfect, she thought, mentally rehearsing what she would say to her parents. They're already sold on the letter— all I need to do is play the part. Enthusiastic, focused, responsible. If they think it's a great opportunity, they won't ask questions.

She could already hear her mom's voice in her head: *"You're going to learn so much, Emily. This is such an amazing experience."* The thought of lying to her parents yet again made her chest tighten. But what choice did she have?

Then there was Sophie. Emily bit her lip, guilt swirling in her gut. Sophie had been her rock, the one person who truly knew the truth. But this… this felt different. Leaving for an entire summer would hurt their friendship, no matter how much she promised to call. She imagined Sophie's hurt expression and the inevitable confrontation.

"Soph, I'm going to England for training. It's a big deal, and I can't pass it up." The words sounded rehearsed, hollow, even in her mind. Sophie deserved more than half-truths, but Emily didn't know how to give it to her without pushing her away.

And then there was Lucas. Her thoughts lingered on him, bringing a mix of warmth and sadness. He'd been so supportive, but the idea of spending months apart filled her with dread. She replayed their earlier conversation, his reassurances echoing in her mind. *"You're going to be amazing. I'll be here when you get back."*

What if he's not? The thought hit her like a punch to the gut. What if I come back, and everything has changed? For a fleeting moment, the idea of quitting the agency entirely flared to life. I could stay here. Finish school. Be with Lucas. Be normal.

Her heart raced at the possibility. She imagined what it would feel like to tell Lucas she was walking away from it all. *"I'm done, Lucas. I just want to be with you."* She pictured his reaction, the way he might pull her into a hug and promise it was the right decision. But deep down, a small, stubborn voice reminded her: This life chose you for a reason. You can't walk away now.

Tears pricked at her eyes as she grappled with the conflicting emotions. The agency, her family, Sophie, Lucas… every piece of her life felt like it was pulling her in a different direction. She didn't know how much longer she could keep all the threads from unraveling.

Her phone buzzed. It was Lucas.

Chapter 21

Emily smiled as she swiped to answer. "Hey, I didn't expect to hear from you tonight."

"Hey," Lucas said, his voice uncharacteristically hesitant. "I… uh, I have some news."

Emily's smile faltered. "What's going on? Are you okay?"

"Yeah, yeah," he rushed to assure her. "I just… this is kind of awkward to say. I just found out that I've been chosen for the academy in England."

Emily froze, her breath catching. "You're going to England?"

"Yeah. It was last minute," he explained. "I… I wasn't sure how to tell you. I didn't want it to seem like I was following you or anything. I know we talked about me staying stateside, and—"

"Lucas, stop," Emily interrupted, unable to hold back her laughter. "I'm going too!"

There was a pause on the other end before Lucas let out a disbelieving chuckle. "Wait, seriously? You're not messing with me?"

"I found out last night," Emily said, grinning. "I was dreading going without you, and now I don't have to."

"Well, that changes everything," Lucas said, his tone lighter now. "Looks like we're going to have the summer of a lifetime."

Emily's excitement bubbled over. "You're right. This is going to be amazing. I can't wait."

The next morning, Emily sat at the kitchen table, her parents sipping their coffee as she mustered the courage to tell them the cover story. She glanced at the official-looking letter the agency had sent and cleared her throat.

"Mom, Dad, I need to talk to you about something," she began.

Her mom's brow furrowed with concern. "What is it, sweetheart?"

Emily took a deep breath. "Remember that summer program I mentioned? The one my school recommended me for? I got in."

There was an awkward silence, then finally her dad cleared

his throat. He set down his coffee, his eyes lighting up. "That's fantastic, Emily! When does it start?"

"In two weeks," she said, sliding the letter across the table. "It's in England."

"England?" her mom echoed, her tone a mix of surprise and apprehension. "For the whole summer?"

"Yes," Emily said quickly, launching into the prepared story. "It's an elite leadership and academic program. They only select a handful of students from around the world. This is a huge opportunity for me."

Her dad read the letter, nodding approvingly. "This looks incredible. You'll learn so much, Emily. And England! What an adventure."

Her mom still looked uncertain. "It's just... so far away. And for so long. Are you sure about this?"

Emily reached across the table, taking her mom's hand. "I know it's a big step, but I really want to do this. It's an opportunity I can't pass up."

After a long pause, her mom finally smiled. "If you're sure, then we support you. You'll have to call us every week."

"I promise," Emily said, relief washing over her.

Later that afternoon, Emily met Sophie at their usual spot in the park. The sun filtered through the trees, casting long shadows on the grass as they sat on the bench.

"Okay, spill it," Sophie said, folding her arms. "You've been acting weird all day."

Emily hesitated, then blurted out, "I'm going to England for the summer."

Sophie's eyes widened. "What? For another mission?"

"No," Emily said quickly. "It's training. The agency selected me for their elite academy."

Sophie's face fell. "The whole summer? What about us? What about… everything?"

"I'll call you as often as I can," Emily promised. "This is a huge deal, Soph. I can't say no."

Sophie looked away, her jaw tight. "I get it. It's just… you're always leaving. And now you're going even farther away."

Emily's heart ached. "I know. I'm sorry. But this is important. Please understand."

After a long silence, Sophie finally sighed. "Fine. Just don't forget about me, okay?"

Emily smiled, squeezing Sophie's hand. "Never."

The next week at school was a blur of final exams and year-end events. Emily tried to focus, but her mind kept drifting to England—and Lucas.

But her excitement was tinged with tension. She noticed a black car parked outside the school one day, the driver was

watching the entrance. When she mentioned it to Lucas during a text exchange, his response was immediate:
Lucas: Keep an eye on it. Let Benson know if it happens again.

The following day, her history teacher, Mr. Callahan, stopped her after class. "Emily, can I talk to you for a second?"
Her heart skipped a beat. "Of course."
He studied her for a moment. "You've been distracted lately. Is everything okay?"
Emily forced a smile. "Just a lot going on. End-of-year stress, you know?"
Mr. Callahan nodded slowly but didn't look entirely convinced. "Well, if you need anything, let me know."
"Thanks," Emily said, quickly leaving the room. Too close, she thought, her pulse racing.

By Friday, the excitement was palpable. Lucas had texted her a countdown: **One week until England.**

Her parents were buzzing about what to pack, Sophie was trying to stay upbeat, and Emily's nerves were a jumble of anticipation and anxiety. As she walked home that afternoon, she couldn't help but wonder: Am I ready for this?
She smiled and finally began to relax when suddenly she

saw Mr. Callahan talking with the man in the black car!

She hurried back inside, ducking behind a row of lockers to watch from the window. The man in the suit handed Mr. Callahan a small envelope before slipping into the car and driving off. Mr. Callahan looked around briefly, his expression unreadable, before heading toward his own car.

Emily's heart pounded. What just happened? She pulled out her phone, texting Lucas immediately.

Emily: Callahan just met with someone suspicious. Black car. Suit. This can't be a coincidence.

Her phone buzzed seconds later.

Lucas: Get out of there. Now. I'll notify Benson. Stay sharp, Em.

As she tucked her phone away, a cold realization hit her. Whatever was going on, it was bigger than she had imagined—and she was right in the middle of it.

Chapter 22

Friday night had barely settled into quiet when Emily's phone buzzed with the agency's alert tone. She sighed, letting her head fall back against her headboard. No rest for the weary. When she saw the alert's priority level—**CRITICAL**—her stomach sank.

A video call from Benson followed almost immediately. Emily propped her phone against a stack of books, her heart thudding in her chest as his stern face appeared on the screen.

"Agent Carter," Benson began, his tone clipped, "we have an urgent situation. This one hits close to home."

Emily straightened. "How close?"

"Your history teacher, Mr. Callahan, has been identified as an active participant in a rogue network targeting national infrastructure. He's working with a known operative—codename: Argus. Their target is the national power grid. If successful, their plan could plunge the country into chaos."

Emily felt a chill crawl up her spine. "What do you need me to do?"

"They're meeting tomorrow night at an abandoned warehouse on the outskirts of town. Your mission is to observe, gather intel, and, if possible, neutralize the threat. We believe the attack is imminent."

"What's my support?" she asked, her voice steady despite her racing thoughts.

Benson's expression softened slightly. "This mission requires discretion. We're authorizing Sophie as a civilian asset. She knows enough to assist you effectively."

Emily hesitated. "Are you sure? I don't want to put her in danger."

"She's your call. If you trust her, use her. You'll need someone on the ground while you're inside."

Emily nodded. "Understood. I'll bring her in."

Benson's face hardened again. "Failure is not an option, Carter. Keep me updated."

The screen went dark, leaving Emily staring at her reflection. This wasn't just a mission—this was personal. Saturday morning, Emily met Sophie at their usual spot in the park. Sophie greeted her with a cheerful wave, but her smile disappeared as she caught Emily's grim expression. "What's going on?" Sophie asked, lowering her voice instinctively.

Emily took a deep breath, knowing there was no easy way to say it. "There's a mission. Here. And I need your help." Sophie blinked. "Here? Like, in town?"

Emily nodded and launched into the explanation. She detailed the intel on Mr. Callahan, the rogue network, and the impending attack. Sophie listened in stunned silence, her fingers gripping the edge of the bench.
"You're serious," Sophie finally said, her voice barely above a whisper. "Mr. Callahan is… involved in this?"
"Yes," Emily said firmly. "And I can't do this alone. I need someone I trust to watch my back."
Sophie hesitated, her face pale. "What exactly do you need me to do?"
"You'll be my lookout," Emily explained. "Stay outside the warehouse and report anything suspicious. I'll be inside gathering evidence."
Sophie swallowed hard, then nodded. "Okay. Let's do this."

By Saturday night, Emily and Sophie were in position. The abandoned warehouse was ahead, its shattered windows and peeling paint casting eerie shadows in the fading light. Emily crouched behind a stack of crates while Sophie watched from a borrowed van parked across the street.

"Anything yet?" Sophie whispered through the earpiece.

"Not yet," Emily replied, scanning the area. "Stay alert."

Minutes later, headlights pierced the darkness. A sleek black car rolled into the lot, and Emily's stomach tightened as Mr. Callahan stepped out, followed by a man in a sharp suit. They carried a briefcase and disappeared into the building.

"I'm going in," Emily said, her voice steady despite the adrenaline coursing through her veins.

"Be careful," Sophie replied, her voice tinged with worry.

Inside, the warehouse was a maze of rusting machinery and empty crates. Emily crept toward the faint sound of voices, her steps silent on the dusty floor. Peering around a corner, she spotted Callahan and the suited man standing over a table covered in blueprints.

"This is it," the suited man said, his voice sharp. "Once the grid goes down, we'll move on the secondary targets. By the time they recover, it'll be too late."

Emily's blood ran cold. A coordinated blackout followed by targeted attacks? She activated her earpiece. "Sophie, record this. We need proof."

"On it," Sophie whispered back.

As Emily leaned closer, her foot brushed against a loose pipe. The clatter echoed through the warehouse like a gunshot.

"Who's there?" Argus barked, pulling out a gun.

Emily froze, her heart pounding. She ducked behind a stack of crates as Callahan and Argus approached.

Before Emily could retreat, Callahan spotted her. "It's her!" he shouted, his voice echoing through the warehouse. "Get her!"

Emily darted out of her hiding spot, her boots slamming against the metal floor as she sprinted for the exit. The suited man pulled a gun, firing off a shot that ricocheted dangerously close to her. She ducked, zigzagging through the machinery, her heart pounding.

The exit loomed ahead, but Callahan was fast, his footsteps closing in. Emily grabbed a rusted chain hanging from the ceiling and swung it back, forcing him to dodge. The distraction gave her just enough time to burst through the side door into the open air.

"Sophie!" she shouted, skidding across the gravel lot.

Sophie was in the driver's seat of the van, her eyes wide with panic as she saw Emily sprinting toward her. "Get in!"

Emily threw herself into the passenger seat just as Callahan and the suited man emerged from the warehouse. Sophie

As Emily leaned closer, her foot brushed against a loose pipe. The clatter echoed through the warehouse like a gunshot.

"Who's there?" Argus barked, pulling out a gun.

Emily froze, her heart pounding. She ducked behind a stack of crates as Callahan and Argus approached.

Before Emily could retreat, Callahan spotted her. "It's her!" he shouted, his voice echoing through the warehouse. "Get her!"

Emily darted out of her hiding spot, her boots slamming against the metal floor as she sprinted for the exit. The suited man pulled a gun, firing off a shot that ricocheted dangerously close to her. She ducked, zigzagging through the machinery, her heart pounding.

The exit loomed ahead, but Callahan was fast, his footsteps closing in. Emily grabbed a rusted chain hanging from the ceiling and swung it back, forcing him to dodge. The distraction gave her just enough time to burst through the side door into the open air.

"Sophie!" she shouted, skidding across the gravel lot.

Sophie was in the driver's seat of the van, her eyes wide with panic as she saw Emily sprinting toward her. "Get in!"

Emily threw herself into the passenger seat just as Callahan and the suited man emerged from the warehouse. Sophie slammed her foot on the gas, the van jerking forward with a screech as they tore out of the lot.

"They're following us!" Sophie yelled, glancing in the rearview mirror. The black sedan was gaining on them, its headlights glaring like twin eyes in the night.

Emily fumbled with her bag, pulling out a smoke bomb. "Hold steady!" She rolled down the window, the wind whipping her face as she tossed the device onto the road. Thick gray smoke billowed out, obscuring the sedan's view.

"Did it work?" Sophie asked, her voice tight with hope.

Emily looked back just in time to see the sedan swerve but recover. "Not for long. Take the next turn!"

Sophie veered onto a narrow side street, the tires screeching. The sedan followed, its engine roaring. Emily's mind raced. They needed to lose the car—and fast.

"There's an alley up ahead," she said, pointing. "We'll ditch the van there."

"What?" Sophie cried. "We're abandoning the van?"

"It's our only chance," Emily said. "Trust me."

Sophie hesitated but nodded. She slammed on the brakes, pulling into the alley. Emily grabbed her arm as they exited the vehicle. "Stay low, and follow me."

The two of them darted down the dark alley, their shadows stretching along the brick walls.

"They're on foot now!" Sophie whispered, her voice trembling.

Emily scanned the area, spotting an old, boarded-up building. She tugged Sophie toward it, prying open a loose plank just wide enough for her friend to slip inside.

"Stay here," Emily said, her tone firm. "You'll be safe."

"What about you?" Sophie asked, her eyes wide with fear.

"I'll lead them away," Emily replied. "Trust me."

Sophie grabbed Emily's arm. "Be careful."

Emily nodded and slipped back into the shadows, her movements silent. She darted through the maze of alleys, leading Callahan and the suited man away from Sophie's hiding spot.

The chase was relentless. Emily scaled a chain-link fence, her arms burning with the effort, just as Callahan rounded the corner. She dropped to the other side, sprinting toward an abandoned rail yard. The sound of their pursuit was deafening—heavy breaths, pounding footsteps, and the occasional shout.

Emily spotted an old train car, its door slightly ajar. She slipped inside, crouching in the dark. Her breath came in short gasps as she listened. The men's voices grew louder.

"She can't have gone far," Callahan growled.

Emily reached into her bag, pulling out a small device.

This will buy me time. She tossed it toward the train car's entrance and covered her ears. The explosion of light and sound disoriented her pursuers, their shouts turning to confusion.

Taking the opportunity, Emily bolted from the train car, heading for the docks. The adrenaline coursing through her veins pushed her forward. As the docks came into view, she spotted Benson's team waiting near a van.

"Over here!" she yelled, waving frantically.

Agents swarmed the area, intercepting Callahan and the suited man just as they stumbled out of the rail yard. The two men fought back, but the agents overpowered them, slamming them against a wall and securing them in cuffs. Emily doubled over, her hands on her knees as she tried to catch her breath. Benson approached, his expression grim.

"Good work, Carter," he said. "You led them straight to us."
Emily straightened, nodding. "And Sophie?"
"She's safe," Benson assured her.
Emily's shoulders sagged with relief.

Chapter 23

The phone buzzed on Emily's nightstand, its glow cutting through the dim light of her room. She grabbed it, her heart leaping when she saw Lucas's name.

"Hey," she said, her voice soft but eager.
"Hey, Em," Lucas replied, his tone warm. "Did I wake you?"
"No," she assured him, settling back against her pillows. "I was just going over my packing list for the academy."
Lucas chuckled, the sound sending a pleasant shiver through her. "Knowing you, it's probably color-coded."
"Of course it is," she teased. "Organization is key when you're saving the world."
"Or when you're trying to impress the best-looking guy in training," he quipped.

Emily laughed, her cheeks warming. "And who might that be?"

"Guess you'll have to wait and see," Lucas said, his voice dipping into a playful tone. "But seriously, I can't wait to spend the summer with you."

Her heart fluttered. "Me too. Though I'm pretty sure they'll keep us too busy to enjoy it."

"Oh, I'll find ways," he replied, a hint of mischief in his voice. "Besides, we're pretty good at improvising."

Emily smiled, her mind flickering to their shared missions, the quick thinking, and the stolen moments in between. "Just don't get us kicked out before we even start."

"No promises," Lucas said, laughing. "Goodnight, Em. Dream of me."

"Goodnight, Lucas," she whispered, the line going quiet but her heart still racing.

The next day, Emily met Sophie at the park. They sat on the grass, their backs against the bench they'd so often occupied.

"So," Sophie began, fiddling with the edge of her shirt. "Is it always like that? The danger, the running, the… bullets?"

Emily winced. "Not always. But yeah, it's not exactly a desk job."

Sophie exhaled, her fingers digging into the grass. "I don't know if I could ever do what you do. I was terrified, Emily. And I wasn't even the one being chased."

Emily placed a reassuring hand on her friend's arm. "You were amazing, Soph. I couldn't have done it without you."
Sophie gave her a small smile. "Benson mentioned something about the agency being interested in me. Like, seriously interested."
Emily's eyebrows shot up. "Really? That's... wow. What did you say?"
"I said I'd think about it," Sophie admitted. "But honestly, I'm not sure I'm cut out for that kind of life."
Emily nodded, understanding the weight of that decision. "It's not for everyone. And it's okay if it's not for you."
Sophie hesitated, then said, "I'm just glad you're okay. That's all that matters to me."
"I'm always careful," Emily promised. "And I'll always have your back, no matter what you decide."

The last week of school was a whirlwind of final exams, year-end assemblies, and bittersweet goodbyes. Emily tried to stay focused, but her thoughts kept drifting to the summer ahead.

On the final day, lockers slammed and laughter echoed through the halls as students celebrated the start of summer. Emily stood by her locker, clearing out the last of her books when Sophie appeared beside her.

"This feels weird," Sophie said, glancing around. "Like everything's changing."

Emily nodded. "It is. But it's not all bad. Change can be good."

Sophie smiled, but it didn't quite reach her eyes. "Just promise me you'll call. I don't want to be one of those friends who drifts away."

Emily closed her locker, turning to face her. "I promise. No matter where I am, you'll always be my best friend."

They hugged tightly, and for a moment, the weight of their separate paths faded.

The weekend was a flurry of activity as Emily packed for the academy. Her room was a mess of clothes, gear, and travel essentials, but she found moments to spend with her parents in between.

Saturday evening, they had a family dinner on the back porch, the scent of grilled burgers filling the air.

"So, England," her dad said, leaning back in his chair. "Are you ready for it?"

Emily nodded, swallowing a bite of food. "I think so. It'll be a big adjustment, but I'm excited."

"We're proud of you," her mom said, her eyes glistening. "You've always been so determined. Please don't forget to call us, okay?"

"I won't," Emily promised. "I'll miss you guys."

Her dad reached over, squeezing her hand. "And we'll miss you. But this is your adventure, Emily. Go make the most of it."

Emily smiled, the warmth of their support settling over her like a blanket—until her mom added casually, "Maybe we'll come visit you this summer. England would be a wonderful trip."

Emily froze, her fork hovering mid-air. "Visit?" she echoed, her voice a pitch higher than normal.

"Why not?" her dad said, grinning. "We've always wanted to go. And we could see you in action at this prestigious program. Meet your teachers. Maybe take you out for a proper English dinner."

Emily's mind raced, panic clawing at her chest. What if they find out? What if the agency slips up? She forced a smile, her palms damp.

"That sounds... great," she said, trying to sound enthusiastic. "But it's a really intensive program. I don't know how much free time I'll have."

Her mom waved a hand. "Oh, we wouldn't get in your way. Just a quick visit. Maybe a weekend."

"We'll see," Emily said quickly, her appetite evaporating. "I'll have to check the schedule."

Her parents exchanged a look, but didn't press further. Emily excused herself soon after, retreating to her room. She sank onto her bed, her heart pounding. *What if they came and saw the truth?* The thought of her carefully constructed double life unraveling made her stomach churn.

She grabbed her phone, texting Lucas.
Emily: Small crisis. Parents want to visit England.
Lucas: What?? That can't happen. What did you say?
Emily: I stalled. But I'm not sure how long that'll work.
Lucas: We'll figure it out. Don't panic, okay?

Emily exhaled slowly, her fingers tightening around her phone. Figure it out. Those words were easier said than done.

Sunday night, as the last of her packing was done, Emily's phone buzzed with a video call from Lucas. She smiled as she answered, his familiar face lighting up the screen.
"Almost ready?" he asked.
"Almost," she replied, sitting on her bed. "What about you?"
"Getting there," he said, then hesitated. "Emily, there's something I need to tell you."
Her smile faltered. "What is it?"
Lucas's expression grew serious. "I overheard something at

the agency. There's a rumor that the training isn't just about preparation. They're using it to vet agents for something bigger. Something dangerous."
Emily's heart sank. "What kind of something?"
Lucas shook his head. "I don't know yet, but whatever it is, it's not good. Just promise me you'll keep your guard up."
"I always do," she said, her voice firm but her mind racing.
"Emily," he said softly, his eyes locking onto hers through the screen. "No matter what happens, we stick together. Right?"
Her chest tightened, the weight of his words pressing down on her. "Right," she whispered.

As the call ended, Emily stared at her phone, her thoughts swirling. The summer ahead was already uncertain, but now it felt like the stakes were higher than ever. And as she turned out the light, one thought lingered in her mind:
What exactly have I signed up for?

Epilogue

The sprawling campus of the elite training academy was more impressive than Emily had imagined. Ancient stone buildings stretched high against the cloudy English sky, their ivy-covered facades exuding both history and secrecy. The grounds buzzed with activity—young agents in crisp uniforms sparred on training mats, while others gathered in clusters, pouring over maps and high-tech gadgets.

Emily adjusted her bag on her shoulder, her nerves tingling with anticipation. This was it. The start of a new chapter. Somewhere across the courtyard, she spotted Lucas. His easy smile cut through the sea of unfamiliar faces, and her heart lifted as he waved.

"Hey, Carter!" he called, striding toward her with a confidence that made her grin despite herself. "Ready to dominate the summer?"

Emily rolled her eyes, but her smile betrayed her. "I'm ready to survive it."

Lucas fell into step beside her, their shoulders brushing. "You'll do more than survive. I've seen you in action, remember?"

"Let's hope the instructors feel the same," she quipped.

They made their way to the orientation hall, where rows of recruits sat in silence as a senior agent took the stage. The agent, a stern-looking woman with piercing blue eyes, scanned the crowd as if memorizing each face.

"Welcome to the agency's elite training program," she began, her voice slicing through the quiet. "Here, you will learn not just to survive, but to lead. Only the best will make it to the end."

The weight of her words settled over the room, and Emily's nerves prickled. Only the best. She glanced at Lucas, who gave her a reassuring nod.

Later that evening, Emily wandered the grounds, drawn to the quiet stillness of the academy's lake. The water mirrored the moonlight, casting silvery ripples that danced in the cool breeze. She leaned against a tree, her mind racing with the day's events.

Her phone buzzed. It was Lucas.

Lucas: Meet me by the lake.

Emily smiled, shaking her head. Of course. She looked around, spotting him approaching from the shadows.

His hands were shoved in his pockets, his expression softer than usual.

"Couldn't wait until tomorrow?" she teased as he stopped beside her.

Lucas shrugged, his smirk returning. "Wanted to make sure you hadn't changed your mind about this whole spy thing."

Emily laughed lightly. "Not yet. But ask me again after tomorrow's drills."

He stepped closer, his voice dropping. "You'll be fine, Em. You're stronger than you think."

For a moment, the world seemed to still. Lucas's hand brushed hers, and the warmth of his touch sent a flutter through her chest. She tilted her head up, meeting his gaze. There was something unspoken in his eyes—something that made her breath hitch.

Just as he leaned in, their proximity electric, a loud ping shattered the moment. Emily's phone vibrated in her pocket. She sighed, pulling it out.

It wasn't Lucas. It was the agency. The message was marked **URGENT. SECURE LOCATION REQUIRED.**

Her stomach dropped as she read the text:

New threat detected. Immediate action required.

Lucas leaned over, reading the message. "What is it?"

"I don't know," Emily whispered, already opening the attached file.

Her blood ran cold as an image filled the screen—a photo of herself and Lucas at the academy gates earlier that day, with a single word beneath it: **TARGETS**.

Her breath caught. "This has to be a mistake."

Lucas's expression darkened. "Or it's not."

A second message appeared: **Agent Carter, report to Command Center immediately. Do not share details.**

Emily looked at Lucas, her pulse hammering. "You're not supposed to know about this."

"Well, too late for that," he said, his jaw tightening. "You're not going alone."

"I don't have a choice," she said, her voice trembling. "Lucas, this is serious."

"So am I," he shot back. "I'm not letting you walk into this blind."

Minutes later, Emily slipped into the Command Center, her nerves stretched taut. The room was dimly lit, its walls lined with screens displaying satellite feeds and intelligence reports. Benson's face appeared on the central monitor.

"Agent Carter," he said, his tone colder than she'd ever heard. "We have a situation."

"I saw the message," she replied. "What's going on?"

Benson's eyes narrowed. "A mole has infiltrated the academy. We intercepted communication indicating that you and Agent Dupont have been marked."

Emily's knees went weak. "Marked for what?"

"Elimination," Benson said flatly. "They know you're here, and they're coming."

The lights in the room flickered, and a sharp alarm blared overhead. Benson's image froze, then distorted before disappearing altogether.
Emily's breath hitched. This isn't a drill.
The door behind her burst open, and Lucas stood there, his expression fierce. "We've got to move. Now."
"How did you—"
"No time," he interrupted, grabbing her hand. "They're here."
The sound of heavy boots echoed down the hallway as shadows shifted against the walls. Emily's heart raced as Lucas pulled her into a side corridor.
"We can't outrun them," she whispered, her voice trembling.
"Then we don't," Lucas said, his grip tightening. "We outsmart them."

By the time they reached the academy's underground tunnels, the alarms had grown distant. Lucas stopped, his breathing ragged, and turned to Emily.
"This doesn't end here," he said, his voice low. "Whoever's behind this, they won't stop until they get what they want."
Emily nodded, her resolve hardening. "Then we don't stop either."

As they disappeared into the shadows, Emily felt the weight of her new reality pressing down. The academy was supposed to be a place of learning, of growth—but now it was a battlefield. And this was only the beginning.

Somewhere in the distance, unseen eyes watched their every move.